OBEAH

by

Carlton J. Rapp
and
Kati S. Rapp

Pittsburgh, PA

ISBN 1-56315-215-0

Paperback Fiction
© Copyright 2000 Carlton and Kati Rapp
All Rights Reserved
First Printing — 2000
Library of Congress #99-65314

Request for information should be addressed to:

SterlingHouse Publisher, Inc.
The Sterling Building
440 Friday Road
Pittsburgh, PA 15209
www.sterlinghousepublisher.com

Cover Design: Michelle S. Vennare — SterlingHouse Publisher, Inc.

Cover Art: The Psychic by Sally Stormon, an original drawing
from the private collection of Thomas S. and Cynthia Sterling

Typesetter: Beth Buckholtz

Printed in Canada

DEDICATION

For Cintra
who will write one of her own one day

For Chandra
who could care less

CHAPTER ONE

"This is not acceptable, Mr. Correy," Singh said as our meeting ended. He was ultra-polite, but pronounced the Mr. as if he were cleaning a dog mess.

I shrugged as I stood to leave. "Just business," I said. "Nothing personal. You've had your quarry for some time. I'm sure you will find another contractor."

I did not tell him he rubbed me the wrong way, that I had disliked him from the moment I entered his office to discuss his proposal to supply gravel and other material for my operations. He was one of those Indians that look like they've baked in the sun too long. He was short, scrawny and almost black in complexion. He wore a look that indicated he thought he was superior to all he met, a haughty, condescending look, with attitude to match. I had met his type before, and I didn't like the type. My reasons for disliking him may not have been logical, but, regardless of the reasons, I had no intention of doing business with someone I did not like. I was well enough established that I could get away with that attitude. Not fair to Singh, but that's how it works sometimes. Charlie, my partner, would probably have struck a deal, but he refused to go to meetings on Saturdays. I moved toward the door of Singh's office. I had a few qualms on my reaction to Singh's physical presence and wanted to leave before I changed my mind.

"Mr. Correy," said Singh, in a soft voice, but it caught my attention and stopped me before I had opened the door.

I turned to face him, once again. He was still at his desk, but standing. I had expected some anger, as my handling of this business had not been something I could be proud of, but what I saw in his eyes, what I sensed, was more than simple anger at not receiving a contract. He was outraged, like a kid accustomed to always having his way suddenly finding himself thwarted. There was also an aura of malevolence, as if he considered such a refusal of his wishes to be worthy of severe punishment. It sounds weird, but this is what I felt from him, and I had learned to trust these intuitions long ago. I abruptly found myself very pleased I had turned his ass down. No more guilt feelings.

"I need this contract," Singh said. "Since I have met all your requirements and had a preliminary approval from your partner, I assumed there would be no problem."

I looked at him. The words were reasonable, and spoken in a soft voice, but the eyes flashed fire. This guy was not used to being turned down and probably had his methods to get back at "locals" who dared displease him. However, I was not a local, I barely knew him, and I had no intention of changing my mind or getting into a shouting match, or what the Trinidad people called a "cuss fight."

"Charlie was wrong," I said. "We don't give preliminary approvals." I turned back to the door. "I'm sorry we couldn't do business," I continued, "but I'm sure there will be other opportunities."

"I will not accept this," Singh growled. "This matter is not yet at an end."

"Wrong," I answered, as I opened the door and moved outside, into the humid oven of downtown Port of Spain. I closed the door as I left.

As I started down the street, I noticed the mid-morning traffic was already starting to build up. However, there was not, yet, enough traffic noise to keep me from hearing Singh's office door opening again. I did not look back immediately, but I felt his eyes on me as I moved quickly to my car. I unlocked the car, finally glancing back.

He was staring at me. For some reason I shivered, suddenly uncomfortable under that steady gaze. Our eyes locked for a moment, then he moved back into his office. I stared at where he had stood, feeling light-headed, as if I had just escaped something serious.

"I'm getting as bad as Jadine," I muttered to myself, as I got in my car, started it, and turned the air conditioning on high.

I wound my way out of the downtown area and got on the road to Maraval. As I passed through Maraval and started the last part of the drive to Maracas, the road narrowed, traffic became a little thinner and a little faster.

At this point I could almost taste the beach at Maracas where Jadine and the kids would be waiting. My sudden case of nerves would definitely not survive Maracas, but, for now, it was still with me. Maracas was where I had met Jadine originally, and the place remained my favorite spot on the island.

I pushed the 1980 Mazda, hoping this would shake off the spooky feeling I had felt since Singh's parting stare at me at his office. It was a therapy that often worked for me. The car was brand new, fire engine red, and a piece of junk, but it could really move. Jadine loved it. My feelings were a little more ambiguous.

Still, piece of junk or jewel of the highway, it was not too smart to push it, so I didn't overdo it. The winding, narrow road which led to Maracas Beach was heavily traveled, with a large assortment of switchbacks and potholes, and Trinidad drivers are not known for careful driving. It was not a road to be negotiated with your mind out of gear. Normally, I loved this drive, with the fantastic parade of rain forest scenes, mountain vistas, waterfalls, and glimpses of distant ocean beaches. Today was no exception, despite my little case of nerves.

I had first found this road about four months after I came to Trinidad to help build the new water supply system that stretched from the rain forests of Oropuche to the treatment plant at Arima. As the job continued, I went to Maracas as often as I could, met Jadine, and married. It then seemed natural to stay here. Since my wife was a native, there were no restrictions to force me to leave at the end of the original job.

Thinking of Jadine calmed me, and I eased on the accelerator. As always. She was the best thing to ever happen to me. My nervousness over Singh began to evaporate, replaced by anticipation. Jadine had come up earlier with Annette, so she would be waiting. Stupid to let Singh bug me, I thought. This is supposed to be a fun day.

I concentrated on the last few switchbacks before reaching the beach area. A small iguana ran from the rain forest across the road, no more than a foot long. I braked, and missed. I hated to hit animals with a car, any kind of animal.

I pulled into the beach parking area and saw her and the kids almost at once. They were wandering across the beach, their heads down. Probably looking for chip chips and pacro, I thought, hoping they were finding some.

I stripped off my outer garments and moved to join them. I didn't see Annette at all.

Jadine spotted me before I reached them. "Clark!" she squealed and ran to meet me. We had several seconds before the kids piled on, and we all ended up in the sand.

It turned out to be the fun day I had originally expected, and I managed to put Singh and all my other problems out of my mind. Annette and her boy friend left early in the afternoon, after our lunch under the coconut trees near the north end, and we never missed them.

We were a tight-knit family. Many of our few friends called us the odd couple. I was six feet in height, slim and typical American, Irish-German extraction. Jadine, in contrast, was less than five feet tall, a pure Trinidad Indian whose grandparents came to Trinidad from India itself. She had long, black hair, brown skin, and a fantastic figure. Jamie was four, barely, and Karen three.

That evening, as some of the heat dissipated, we lay on a blanket near the ocean, under the coconut trees, watching the children play. It was very peaceful.

"How was the meeting?" Jadine asked.

I looked at her, grinned. She had been dying to ask the question all day. "Not too bad," I said. "I didn't handle things all that great, but I think I made the right decision. Singh wasn't too happy about it though."

"Singh?" she asked. "Which Singh?" Her voice was cooler, almost forced.

I noticed the voice change, saw the sudden concern in her face. "Yeah, Singh," I answered. "Patel, I think. He owns that new quarry up in the Northern Range, where I built all those little package water plants for WASA, the Water and Sewerage Authority."

"He workin' with you?" she asked.

"No," I answered. "That's what I meant when I said I didn't do a great job on the meeting. I think I might have insulted him a bit. No big deal, though. He struck me as an asshole, anyhow. Why? You know him or something?"

"He Obeah," she said. "Big shot. What you say to he, what kind of insult you drop on he?"

I started to laugh, to kid her, but seeing the look on her face changed my mind. I remembered the feeling the guy had raised in me. I shrugged, described the meeting to her, including how I turned him down, mostly because he rubbed me wrong. I described his actions, how he had handled not getting the contract.

"Clark, boy, Singh a nasty man to drop insult on. He top Obeah man this area, and Uncle Krishna say he kill people who mess up he business deals." She mentioned several ugly murders I had read about in the *Guardian* and said her uncle thought Singh was involved.

"Then you should be glad I turned his ass down," I said, when finally I found an opening in her monologue.

Jadine gave me a look that shut me up. "Don' be foolish," she said. "Singh, he big time Obeah. He deal with spirits and demon and them. He don' do small thing. He raise he own special chicken and goat for sacrifice and thing, and he make real trouble."

"Jadine," I said. "I respect your beliefs on this Obeah, but Americans aren't into this stuff like you people here in Trinidad. This Singh thought I'd know his reputation and jump over my own asshole to do what he wanted. If he thinks I'm going to get spooked by some dead chicken mumbo-jumbo, he's got another think coming."

Jadine looked at me, concern and resignation in her face. "All these years in Trinidad, and you still don' believe. Never mind, it dark now, and we need to go home. What's done is done, and no taking back."

I started to speak, but she hushed me.

"Forget it," she said. "We just hope for best, and try to handle if worst happen. Too late to change."

We got busy loading up. The full moon was riding high when we finally were in the car and on our way home.

The kids conked out quickly, sprawled across the back seat. Jadine snuggled next to me, and we moved slowly down the almost deserted road.

Halfway to Maraval, Jadine stiffened. "Something wrong," she said. She glanced behind us, brought her gaze forward again.

"Like what?" I asked, looking in the rear-view mirror at the empty road behind us.

"Not real," she answered.

She was always doing this to me; she claimed she could sense the spirit world, and she was very attuned to the supernatural. Not that I could fault her, for she had proven correct in her intuitions and observations too often to slough it off. I just didn't believe there was a supernatural source for her feelings and sudden insights.

I found I was a little spooked. I flexed my left arm, absently rubbed it a little, a nervous reaction I had been catching myself at the past few months. The doctor had warned me this might happen. It was a direct result of my high blood pressure. I could blame my temper for most of it, but, at least, I had medication to slow things down now. My pressure seemed to get worse last week when my two youngest children from my previous marriage were in a car accident back in the States. My frustration when trying to get information had fixed me up. Again, nothing I could do. I watched Jadine, saw she remained tense.

"What is it?" I asked, curious and a little wary. The night had changed after her terse comments. It did not seem quite so friendly now.

"You don' believe me," she accused.

I took a deep breath, exasperated. "How can I believe you or not believe you if I don't know what you're talking about."

She looked at me, trying to see if I were poking fun at her. I used to do that, before I saw some of the things happen she had seen well in advance.

My move, I thought. "Okay, Jadine, what's going on?" I asked, trying to keep my irritation from showing. That, I knew, would be a mistake.

"Big dog," she answered. "Following we."

I looked in the mirror again. "I don't see anything," I said.

"Don' want you to see he," she answered. "He there, right behind we."

"So what do you want me to do?" I asked. These situations always left me uncomfortable.

"Just get we home," she said. "Touch the gas a little. We almost parked up." She was very agitated. This thing was bugging hell out of her.

I checked the mirror again, nervously, catching her mood. Nothing. I increased our speed as much as the winding road would allow.

She said nothing more for a while, just sat there tense and unhappy. Finally, a few miles from home, she relaxed. "Gone," she said. "I 'fraid he follow we home, but he gone now."

By the time we pulled in the space under our house, in Diego Martin, she was nervous again. Jamie was awake, and could walk in. I picked up Karen with one hand, and the chip chips with the other.

Jadine got the towels and such. We moved up the outside steps. I fumbled the key in the lock and got the door open. I started to go inside, but Jadine stopped me with one hand.

"Back in," she directed. I had been through this drill before. She felt backing in would keep "things" out of the house.

Obediently, I did as I was told. We then put the kids to bed and turned on the television. News. I hadn't realized it was so late. We moved to the couch, and Jadine snuggled into my arms.

"Something follow we home," she announced. "I thought we get away, but I wrong."

I said nothing. Everything was quiet. I felt myself dozing off.

*　*　*

I saw a large dog sitting on the rug, watching us. There was something wrong with the eyes.

Has to be a dream, I thought. If it were, my efforts to wake up were useless. I stared at the dog, daring it to do anything, anything at all. Then I felt something else, a presence, maybe more.

"He going to be vex," came a voice.

"Not we fault," answered a second voice. "How it be we fault if he don' see we? Can' even touch he. Shit."

"He still going to be vex," insisted the first voice. "You know Mr. Singh. He no go by reason and thing."

"So let Fido handle it," was the answer. The dog seemed to perk his ears up a little, gave a doggy grin. The eyes were red, and there still seemed to be something about them, something unusual.

"You know Fido don' do shit if we no start it," stated dream voice number one. "So now what we do? You want to tell he? You want to tell Mr. Singh?"

"No choice, man," came the second voice.

"How 'bout she?" asked number one. "She from here. No way she won' see we. Maybe we fix she, then Mr. Singh he no get quite so vex."

"Better not," came the answer. "Mr. Singh, he say just the white man."

The phone rang and I woke up. Completely. No dog, no voices, no nothing. Jadine answered the phone. Wrong number.

By this time I was wide awake, pouring sweat. My heart pounded.

"What the shit is going on?" I muttered to myself.

Jadine looked at me, picking up on my almost soundless remark. She returned to the couch, worry on her face.

"Saw your dog," I said, and watched fear join the worry. "Easy, babe," I said, quickly. "I'm okay. I was just dreaming."

She was not reassured, her expression remained unchanged. I had a sense of foreboding, like I had crossed an invisible line into very dangerous territory. I was suddenly fearful for my family and myself.

"We go bed," Jadine said, watching me.

"Yeah," I answered.

*   *   *

I was not in my bed. I was not home. Through the thick fog I barely saw a shape to one side. I moved that way, cautious, every sense alert.

It was that damn dog again! As I moved closer, he just sat still, staring at me, his teeth half bared in that doggie grin. Now what, I wondered. The dog got up, moved off in the fog. I followed.

I saw a faint flickering in the distance. As I came closer, I could see a bottle torch guttering fire. Near it was a black chicken head, with the feet below. No body, no support. The thing's eyes followed me as I moved past.

"Another dream," I muttered, disgusted. "Has to be another stupid dream."

I heard faint sounds ahead of me. Singh. He was sitting cross-legged on the ground, barely visible in the fog. The dog was now sitting next to him. He was intoning what sounded like prayers in a singsong voice. I moved forward again, and he looked up, looked straight at me.

He grinned. "I should have told you I was a very nasty person," he said. "Perhaps, as an American, you prefer the term dangerous." He cocked his head to one side. "My friends tell me you could not see them earlier. Most unfortunate. I will have to punish them for their incompetence, of course. You appear to be visualizing suitably now. Perhaps we can discuss why you should be resistant to normal persuasion."

"I have nothing to say to you," I snapped. Seeing Singh had taken the magic out of the scene, rekindled my anger.

"Oh, excellent," came the reply. "He walks, he talks, he makes funny noises. Mr. Correy, I came because you were so inconsiderate and rude at our meeting, and you have failed to advance my business goals. Unless you change your attitude, I shall dispense with you and go to your partner."

"I'm the senior partner," I said, struck by the weirdness of such a conversation in such a setting.

"Not if you are dead," came the answer. "Of course, I could modify the situation by taking action against your family." He stopped, became thoughtful for a moment. "No," he continued, "you would have more value to me after I have terminated your present existence. In such a case your family may still be of some use. Unless you do as I require, of course."

"Touch Jadine or the kids and I'll kill you," I growled.

"You must be alive to deliver on such a threat," Singh answered in a soft voice, "and continued life is dependent on your usefulness."

This bullshit has to stop, I thought. I moved toward him, aching to get my hands on him. The distance between us did not change.

"Sorry," he murmured. "I control this setting. You are here only to hear my comments."

"Bastard," I muttered. I tried again to move, no luck.

His grin was wider than ever, and the dog seemed to have an identical grin. "I wanted you to know what was happening," he said. "As I said, if you continue to deny me, I will have you killed, for you might be of more use to me dead than alive. In fact, your death might be the beginning of a long and prosperous relationship."

I stared at him. "What the hell are you talking about?" I demanded. "You are one ignorant freak. A little dried up piece of shit like you is going to play hell trying to hurt me, let alone kill me."

"We shall see," he answered. "Now I feel it is time to end this conversation." He got up to leave.

"Wait a minute," I said.

He looked at me a moment, then left without another word. The dog grinned and followed him. The chicken head and its attendant parts disappeared.

No. I refused to wake up.

I stumbled through the fog, forcing progress by sheer willpower. I tripped, I stumbled, I kept pushing. Finally, I saw him in the distance, the dog by his side. Slowly the distance narrowed.

The dog noticed me, growled, a deep rumbling that sent shivers down my back. Singh looked at the dog, then looked at me, startled.

"So, he can make waves," he said, almost in a whisper. He gestured at me. "Come," he barked.

I was suddenly in front of him, with no control on my movements. His grin was back, a very nasty grin. "Perhaps an object lesson before we part, so you will understand our relationship to each other. You see, I am not under the restrictions my sendings encountered."

He chuckled, as if at a joke, and reached his hand out to my rigid, unmoving body. His outstretched fingers went through my chest. I felt pain, a terrible pain.

"The heart is a delicate thing," he continued, conversationally. "All I need do is lightly stroke, and you are distressed. How much more distressed if I were to envelop it with my fingers, and squeeze." His hand moved. White pain blurred my vision.

He moved back. The pressure eased. "No," he murmured. "It would be pleasurable, but I have other plans. I do not want your passing to be so easy." Again he moved to leave. "I would not advise you to follow me," he said.

I stared as he disappeared into the fog. Fear had overwhelmed my anger, and I made no move to follow.

Then I felt myself waking up, and the piercing pain in my chest brought me the rest of the way. I lay very still for several minutes, and the pain slowly abated.

It was a long time before I fell asleep again.

* * *

Jadine was still worried when we got up, but I didn't let it bother me. The whole business had been unsettling, but it was just dreams and nerves.

I was in a good mood, the bright early morning sunshine dispersing the fears of the night. "I'm going to get the Sunday paper," I called to Jadine.

"Be careful," she called back.

I started the car, my mind already preoccupied with my plans for the day. As I touched the gas pedal, the dog came through the windshield. He didn't break it, he just came through as if it didn't exist, and sat on the front seat. My foot reflexively pushed on the gas, hard, and the car shot forward, crossed the road, and slammed into the big tree opposite my house.

I went through the windshield, the hard way. As I lost consciousness, I felt a terrible pain in my chest that almost wiped out the pain in my head from breaking the windshield.

I heard a voice, angry. "I told you it wasn't to end yet! I wanted that contract."

Everything went black.

CHAPTER TWO

I swayed a little, a wave of dizziness washed over me. Confused, I looked around. I was standing next to a car. The car was deeply involved with a tree, with which it had obviously just had a losing argument. I thought the car looked familiar, then slowly became aware it was my car.

What the hell is going on, I wondered. I heard agitated voices as neighbors converged on the scene. We had good neighbors, and they were not afraid to be involved. I saw what looked like a body hanging half in the car and half out. In my confusion I had missed that.

"Oh shit!" I cried, and moved to see who it was, and to see if I could help. "Please," I moaned, softly. "Not Jadine."

It was not Jadine, it was a man. "What's he doing in my car," I growled.

I heard Jadine's voice as she came down our stairs. I had moved next to the body, but could not bring myself to look at the face. "Oh God," she cried. "Clark crash we car."

Then she reached the bottom of our steps and was running. "Clark!" she screamed, and ran straight to the body hanging through the windshield.

"I'm here, babe," I said. "I'm okay. I don't know who's in the car."

She ignored me, or didn't hear me, and started hugging the body, and moaning. "Someone call ambulance," she screamed, panic edging into her voice. "Please."

"Easy," I said. "I'm right here. That's not me." I reached toward her, and my hand went right through her.

I stopped. I looked at the body, and saw my own face staring blankly back at me, the eyes wide. "Oh boy," I said.

The neighbors joined my wife, with comments, condolences. Neither they nor Jadine seemed to see me, all they saw was that body, and I knew that if I were standing here, then that body could not be alive.

I could not remember the crash, I could not remember dying, I could not even remember what happened to make me lose control, for it was obvious I had lost control. I did remember telling Jadine I was going to get the paper, and walking out the door.

Did Singh sabotage my car, I wondered. But no, that would not be his style. He'd do something more direct. Plain old accident, I thought. I wondered if I would ever remember exactly what happened.

Then I did remember, suddenly and completely. The dog, the crash, the chest pain, the angry voice.

I sat down, staring at the unpleasant scene before me. I couldn't stay on my feet, My feelings were overwhelming me, and the reality of what had happened was sinking in.

Jadine. I looked at her with horror and compassion and anguish as I watched her bullying the people around her to get help, help that would be too late. She couldn't help my body, and I couldn't help her. I heard a distant siren. Several people were leaving with guilty looks, but still leaving. Don't want to stick around a dead body, I realized. This was Trinidad, and death meant more to these people than to Americans. They did not think death was an ending. I looked at my body again, startled. Right, I thought, but what good does it do if you can't be seen or touched. Might as well be a piece of rock.

I watched Jadine, tears pouring down my face, tears to match those rolling down her cheeks. I trembled. I still could not stand.

Suddenly, I knew Jadine was pregnant. It was a mystery as to how I knew, other than sensing a second life force within her. She had never said a word, maybe didn't know herself, but it was there. I was dead, but I had left part of me with her. I would not be there to help her with this one. Will she want it, because it comes from me? Or will it just be a burden?

She collapsed over the body, moaning softly and crying, sliding to the ground next to the car. Others moved closer, talking to her, comforting her. The ambulance sounds were louder, not more than a block or two away. I hovered nearby, wanted desperately to help her. I wanted her to feel my presence, to know part of me was still around. I wanted to make the horror go away for her.

I almost got through once. She sat up, staring at where I stood, as if she saw me. Then her grief took over once more.

She was still there, on the ground, half sitting and supported by two neighbors on either side, when the ambulance arrived. She stood, like a sleepwalker, and waited for the ambulance attendants.

There were two of them. They moved to my body, took a cursory glimpse, looked at each other.

"Sorry, lady," said one. "He don' need an ambulance, you know. Not this one. He dead."

The second one asked, "Want we to take he anyhow? Don' really make sense. You have to pick he body up at the hospital then. He already here so why go to big bother and thing. Call somebody that help with dead people, we just help with live ones."

"Your choice, lady," added the first one. "You say take, we take. You say no take, we no take. Makes no nevermind to we."

"No," she answered softly. "Just leave me."

"You have to get a doctor," said the second man. "For the death certificate and thing."

"I know," came her answer, a little impatience showing. "Leave me now."

"You have to get he inside," insisted the first man, following a set routine. "You can keep he here a little while, but he have to be inside, and you need to call funeral home so everything legal and thing. Or we can drop he at funeral home. Not supposed to, but we help that way now and then." He waited. He would not leave until he was sure all rules were followed.

"I want he here," she answered, her tears back in force again. "Then I want to be alone with he. Don' worry, boy, I send he to home and thing before dark. You think I stupid? You think I crazy?" She hesitated, then said, "Can you move he inside for me?"

Both nodded agreement and moved my body into the house. They left, the ambulance left, a few friends stayed. Jadine moved to the telephone and called her uncle, Krishna Latchman. He agreed to come right over. I could hear his voice as he talked to Jadine on the phone. Then she called the funeral home.

She sat on the couch and stared at my body on the other couch, tears flowing down her cheeks. From one bedroom came the sound of Jamie crying in his sleep. It was still that early, and the kids would soon wake up to a brand new world.

Jamie stopped crying.

There was no other sound in the house. It sounds weird, but I found the quiet to be deafening in its impact.

Jadine moved to the phone again, and dialed. "Hello? Charles? I need help. Clark is dead, accident and thing." There was a long pause. I assumed Charlie was talking. "All right," she said. "Just knock. Thanks, boy, thanks plenty." She hung up.

Charlie was my business partner and a good friend. I felt better after she made that call, knowing he would help. I had given him some details of my insurance, and Jadine knew where the papers were filed. Once she gave him the papers, he could do what was necessary. Charlie would handle the practical side, and Jadine's uncle could help her on the emotional side.

I relaxed, a little. Then, for the first time, I considered my own position.

I had considered death, when I thought of it at all, as an ending, a finish, a nothing. I had never been convinced there was an afterlife. I thought death would be a clean break, that I would just cease, that there would be no more "me" to perceive anything, that I would end.

Finis! Sure! Instead, I was still here, out of contact with the real world, but still here. There was no blackness, no heaven or hell, just here, in the same old place. I was a ghost, something I had never believed in.

I looked at myself. I looked substantial enough, but Jadine did not see me. I had to walk to reach a new location. I could see, I could hear, I could think.

But can I really do anything? I moved to the front door and tried to open it. I had to exert every ounce of my strength to turn the knob; but, finally exhausted, I stood back and stared at the door, which stood open an inch or so.

So! With a lot of effort, I can make myself noticed. The amount of effort was a little worrisome, though. Then I remembered Jadine had locked the door. I looked and saw the lock was still in place, but the door was open. I tried to close it again, but failed. I stared at that undamaged lock, shook my head.

Jadine walked into the room, stopped short when she saw the open door. "Thought I closed it," she muttered.

As she reached for the door, there stood her uncle, a tall, slender, Indian man. She was briefly startled, then hugged him and pulled him into the house, explaining what had happened to me. The door was forgotten.

Krishna took two neighbors and walked past, with Jadine, and moved my body to the spare bedroom, the guest room, the room we had never used. I followed, unwilling to let Jadine out of my sight. I felt she was my last contact with the world of the living. I had to follow her.

They undressed my body, then cleaned it off and dressed the corpse again, using the new suit I bought last week. I walked over and looked at myself. Don't he look natural, I thought, and stifled the urge to giggle.

Jadine and Krishna went into the children's room. Again I followed.

As soon as I walked in, both Karen and Jamie woke up and started screaming. I knew they did not see me, but obviously they sensed something was wrong.

Jadine hushed them, loved them up, and the tears stopped. I stared at the three of them, my heart yearning for them, my arms aching to comfort them. I wept to myself for the life I no longer had, for the family I left behind. I grieved my own passing.

Then Jadine looked at me, through me. "Clark? You there?" She shivered, reached a hand toward me, then stopped, closed her eyes and clenched her fists. "I must stop this. He not here. He dead! He gone! Forever! Til death do we part. And Death, he come for real."

Krishna stood to one side, watching, saying nothing.

Jadine opened her eyes. I reached to her, but she did not respond. I was not sure, but there had been a few seconds there, a fleeting instant. There had been contact.

Then she said, "Clark, if you there, remember I loved you. Remember that, boy, I loved you."

"I still love you!" I cried.

She did not hear me. Any contact that there had been was now gone.

I heard a minor commotion outside the house. At least two cars had pulled up in front. I listened. There was a knock at the door.

I followed as she answered the door, admitted Charlie along with the doctor.

"Where is he?" Charlie asked.

"The spare bedroom. We already dressed he."

Jadine then led them to my body, stood to one side while the doctor made a cursory check. He straightened, signed the death certificate, and left after a brief word to Jadine to remind her that she had to contact a funeral home. She told him she had already done this.

Jadine now returned her attention to Charlie. He was about my height but weighed almost two hundred fifty pounds. Charlie was the stolid type, the sort of person that inspires trust. He was good people.

"How did it happen?" Charlie asked.

Jadine's control snapped, as she told Charlie her story, and she started crying, heaving rasping sobs. Uneasily, Charlie led her to the couch, sat her down, and patted her shoulder. Krishna remained standing, also ill at ease.

"I'll make all the arrangements for you," Charlie said. "You'll want the body at the funeral home and the wake here, I suppose." He looked at both Jadine and Krishna.

"Yes," Jadine answered.

"All right," Charlie continued. "After the funeral, we'll have to take care of the insurance. The house is in your name?"

"Yes. Oh, please, Charles, not now. Just sit and keep me company. Please, just for now, for a little while. All that other we can take care of later. Please, boy."

He shrugged and sat. He was obviously uncomfortable, but he could not ignore Jadine's tearful request. The long minutes eased past. Karen cried, wanting some water or something. Someone took care of it. Quiet returned, and the long, slow passage of time.

Finally, it was afternoon. The kids had gotten up and were playing quietly, subdued by their mother's mood.

The funeral home people arrived, and my body was taken away. Charlie talked briefly with Jadine and then left. He was glad to leave as he always felt awkward at these things. Jadine almost broke down at that point, but Krishna stayed close and there was no problem. Jadine sat with Krishna for a while, talking. I stayed close that night, the night of my wake. Other neighbors and friends and family began to arrive, to help her cope with her loss.

She knew I was there.

*   *   *

The funeral was on Tuesday. After the funeral service, I rode in the car following the hearse, with Jadine, to the Western Cemetery in

St. James. The place was not large, and the low block wall surrounding it made it look ancient. The cemetery was tucked in a corner at the foot of Fort George Mountain. I stood with Jadine as the coffin was lowered. I felt a strong urge to stay with the coffin, but I resisted.

Somewhere in me there was a voice saying there was still something for me to do here, in the world of the living. Either my family was in trouble they were not yet aware of or Fate was about to administer some new blow. In any event, I had the distinct conviction I could make a difference, even dead.

I was very uncomfortable during the short graveside service. I detected presences in the cemetery; it was not empty. It was nothing tangible, but it was undeniable, and I was not yet ready for that. I was too recently alive. It was little things, like a swirl of movement near a tombstone, a flutter of wings with nothing to be seen, a sudden chill in the air, wind gusts. Everything felt contrived, as if something were trying to get my attention, but I saw and heard nothing substantial, nothing measurable.

I noticed several visitors I did not know. One was a well-dressed guy, Indian by his facial characteristics. Is he a friend of Singh, I wondered. However, I couldn't see why Singh should be interested. I mean, he wanted me dead, I was dead, end of story. There were two black guys with this first character. They looked pretty scruffy, and one appeared to have a problem with his head. They left early. I don't believe Jadine noticed them.

I looked at the flowers, at the name tags. There was a large expensive bouquet from Singh. I seethed, but the bouquet stayed where it was. The unwanted visitors, the hints of other unseen visitors, the bouquet, all combined to make me very nervous I had a feeling Singh had meant for me personally to see those flowers, the dead me, and that he fully expected me to be able to see them. He was tormenting softly, even after my death.

I left the cemetery with Jadine, and I was glad to leave. I wandered around the house, watching and waiting. Something was going to happen. I felt sure of this.

I waited.

CHAPTER THREE

Jadine went to the bank four weeks later, on a Thursday, to take care of the insurance. I had been very pleasantly surprised that the check had been so prompt, and I suspected Charlie had visited the insurance claims office personally on his last trip to the States.

In any event, Jadine received the check, arranged for a babysitter, and left for the bank. Following some inner urge, I went with her. Since Jadine could not read or write all that well, I was afraid that her weakness might encourage somebody to take advantage.

Charlie had already sent the trust fund papers to the bank. All Jadine had to do was go to the bank with the check, and the bank would take care of the rest. I had arranged for a trust account which would furnish her with forty thousand Trinidad dollars per year for a great many years, with limited access to emergency funds if approved by a bank-appointed trustee. With forty thousand a year and her own house, she would not be badly off, even if she never worked a day in her life.

So why am I here, I wondered. What's got me so worried? Why are my nerves on edge?

When her identity was verified, the bank notified the vice president who had been assigned to handle Jadine's account. His name was Maharaj. I followed Jadine to the little cubicle that served as his office and watched as he made explanations and presented new papers for her signature.

All my mental alarms went off, for there should have been no new papers. None.

"I don' understand, Mr. Maharaj. I was told no changes."

Good, I thought. Hang onto that. This character is up to something!

"Mrs. Correy, this is my business, this is what I do for a living, and I'm good at what I do. Who set up these papers and told you what to do? Your husband?"

"Yes. My husband and he partner, Mr. Charles Emby."

I walked over and looked at his nameplate, wanting to know his first name. Chanho. He was Chanho Maharaj.

"Ah yes," he was saying, "another American. My dear Mrs. Correy, you have been advised by two Americans. They have done a very good job, but they are not familiar with all the necessary statutes in this country. There are additional taxes which were not taken into consideration, and there are bank fees that have been incurred. Now, please look at these forms. It is obvious—"

I tuned that smooth obnoxious voice out, furious. This Chanho Maharaj had somehow discovered Jadine's true aptitude, so far as reading was concerned, and had determined to take full advantage of it.

He was Indian, he was a vice president in his bank, he was considered a man of importance, above reproach. He was almost white in complexion, but he was pure Indian. He was not much taller than Jadine, but he was rather plump. He sported a miniscule moustache, the kind that looks like it was drawn with a pencil. He looked eminently trustworthy.

I looked at the papers, the supposed tax papers and various affidavits. They were forms which bilked Jadine of two hundred thousand dollars, Trinidad currency, for Maharaj's private account. He already had his own deposit slip made out to deposit his new-found wealth without delay. I assume he limited himself only so his superiors would not realize something was wrong.

Because she could not read well, and Charlie was not able to come with her, Jadine would have to accept what the little bank man told her. After all, she had no reason to doubt someone so high in the bank's hierarchy, and the little bastard oozed confidence and respectability out of every pore.

All I could do was watch. I could do nothing else.

"Now, Mrs. Correy," he was saying, "if you will just sign the insurance check and sign these forms for me, right where I have placed the X, then we can complete our business."

"Maybe I should let Charles see these first."

"That is up to you, of course. All I have done is correct a few errors on the original papers, to bring them in conformance with current Trinidad banking statutes. You will only be wasting the man's time."

Jadine wavered.

Maharaj pushed the papers in front of her, placed a pen in her hand.

He allowed a trace of impatience to escape. "Please, Mrs. Correy, I have a busy day ahead of me. You are not my only responsibility."

Jadine looked about, helplessly, as if she might find me there to advise her. She shrugged. "All right, I sign. Have to trust some times." She signed, returned the check, forms, and pen to Maharaj.

I fumed; I cursed; I yelled. I might as well not have bothered. I was completely helpless.

When finally Jadine stood, to be escorted by Maharaj to the door, I did not move. I stayed with Maharaj and watched my wife go out the door. What hurt most was that she was not aware she had been cheated.

Later, when Chanho Maharaj started home from work, chortling to himself over his good fortune that day, I went with him. I was not sure what, if anything, I could do. I did not know if "haunting" him were even possible, or if I could do it. If it were possible, Maharaj was in for one hell of a spell of it.

I watched him as he drove, as he hummed some Indian tune of some kind and grinned foolishly. He was so happy and excited he made me sick. The passage of time was only getting me pissed, and more obsessed with doing something.

My whole existence now seemed rooted around my desire that this greasy pig of a vice president pay back every cent he had stolen, and I wanted him to pay it personally. If returning it caused him any trouble, that would simply be a bonus.

He must have been aware of my presence on some subconscious level, for when he arrived home to his large, very fancy, two-story mansion in St. James, he opened his car trunk and removed a machete. Following a procedure I had seen Jadine use on several occasions, he backed into his own doorway, cursing and swinging the weapon. I listened appreciatively. Trinidadians are very colorful when it comes to cursing, and Maharaj was no slouch.

I laughed a little, seeing his routine as rather ridiculous. Does he expect this to do any good? To my surprise, I found I could not follow him inside.

Finally a young boy, twelve or so, approached and opened the door. I was inside before Maharaj could repeat his protection spell, or whatever the hell it was. If he still sensed me, he did not show it. I guess the whole business of the machete and the cursing had been "just in case", like knocking on wood in America.

The boy went upstairs. I assumed he was Maharaj's son, and lived here.

Maharaj had settled down to read his newspaper with a stiff drink in his hand. He was very much at peace with his world. I sat next to him, trying to convey my presence to him. Nothing happened. Irritated, I watched him and his family go through everyday movements and finally ready themselves for bed.

As I watched, I remembered Jadine telling me how spirits can tackle the living easiest through dreams, and I remembered my own dream experiences just before I died. Based on these recollections I thought something might be possible.

As the family went to their beds, I followed Maharaj. I watched with interest as he made love to his wife, then rolled over to sleep while she read.

I concentrated, trying to detect his dreams, wanting to get at him and not knowing how to do it. The only thing my concentrated attentions managed was to wake him around three in the morning.

He woke suddenly and completely, his eyes wide and his nose wrinkling. He jumped out of bed.

"I smell rotten meat!" he yelled. "Mandi! Wake up! There's something stink in the house. Something dead!"

Mandi woke, ran to the linen closet just outside the bedroom, grabbed a broom. She returned, and began to wave the broom around as if battling some invisible antagonist from corner to corner. Both she and her husband began praying loudly. I watched, impressed by the performance, but I could not see where anything they were doing had any effect on me.

So not all the superstitions work, I thought.

My smugness did not last long. Mandi started reciting a new round of Indian prayers, and I found myself propelled from the room. My efforts were over for the night. I was not discouraged. On the contrary, I was elated, for the wake up and the prayer bit proved I had accomplished something. I had awakened him from a sound sleep, and I had thrown a scare into him.

As I was ejected into the hallway, I saw the boy peeking, round-eyed, from his room. I didn't see him again later, so I guess he went back to bed.

I had tried for the ultimate confrontation too soon. I'll have to soften him up first, I thought. Maybe some conventional haunting to get him more responsive. Then I can try for a dream again. If he's halfway expecting me, it should make it easier.

I was assuming that this business with the dreams was something that would allow me to communicate, and that was what I wanted. Communication. I didn't think the prayer thing would keep me out of Maharaj's bedroom long, but I did not care at this point. I was not ready yet, so let him think he's safe.

I'm not sure why I thought the prayers were only a temporary thing. It was just a feeling, but it was a feeling laced with certainty. I had been dead less than two months, but I was very much aware that such feelings were more often to be trusted than conventional wisdom practiced by the living.

I rummaged through my recollections of supernatural things, sorting out some of these for testing. How this knowledge had managed to cross the gulf to the world of the living was immaterial. The important fact was that there was contact between the worlds of life and death. Knowing this was enough. Since contact was possible, I was going to make that contact.

I looked at Maharaj's bedroom, grinning. Just wait, asshole, I thought. You're in deep shit, American style.

I resolved to experiment, to see what I could do. I rubbed one foot on the rug leading to his bedroom, then reached down and exerted my strength to raise one edge about three inches into the air. It stayed where I put it.

Satisfied, I moved to the kitchen, and managed after four or five minutes of effort to open the refrigerator door. I remembered what Jadine had told me about spirits spoiling certain types of food, like meat and milk. I stirred my finger around in a large bowl of leftover curry chicken, then tasted my finger.

Stupid! I thought. Dead people can't taste.

I looked at the curry. There was no apparent change. I extended the same finger that had just been in my mouth to stir the curry once again. The food discolored, bubbled. Encouraged, I did the same to the open container of milk. Again, success. Touch, taste, touch. Silly, but it worked.

Hope you enjoy your curry, I thought.

After groping through all the open containers I found, I left the refrigerator. I left the kitchen to turn on the television. The only immediate result was the sign-off symbol. I turned the volume to high, knowing that, later, the station would add music to the logo, but the static might be enough.

I laughed. True, the little bastard hadn't gotten up again, but the television was potentially very noisy. No music yet, but even the static can be irritating. He seemed able to ignore that, so I looked around for something else to play with. I even giggled once, something I almost never do. I was so wound up and expectant that I felt ready to explode.

Seeing nothing inside the house, I moved to the back door to torment the sleeping dog just outside. He barked as I approached, so I moved nearer yet until he became frantic. This was the sort of noise no home owner could ignore.

I heard the bedroom door open. The boy's door opened, also, but he stayed in his room. Maharaj came out.

He immediately tripped on the rug and went flying. He stood up, cursing, yelled at the dog and saw the television was on. He turned it off, stumbled to the kitchen for a drink of milk which he soon spit out in the sink with more cursing. Then he wrinkled his nose, smelling the rotten chicken curry. He returned to the open refrigerator, hunted around until he found the curry and moved outside to throw it over his fence into his neighbor's back yard. Finally, he started back to his bedroom, muttering prayers and curses indiscriminately as he went.

I was thrilled at the extent of my success. I followed him back to his bedroom, unaffected by any of his muttering. He tried to sleep again, but he was still awake as the first light of dawn filtered through his bedroom curtains. He gazed blankly through the window, then the vacant expression turned thoughtful. He shook his wife's shoulder slightly. Her eyes opened.

"Mandi," he said. "You have to call your cousin this morning, the pundit."

"You woke me for that?" she asked.

"Mandi, something is tackling me heavy. We need help."

"My cousin is not that good," she answered. "Maybe we should call someone that knows what to do. I heard the noise you were making out there."

"Your cousin. He's cheaper."

Right on, I thought. I'll fix up the cousin, too.

"All right Chanho," she answered. "I'll call him later, after we're up for the day. Let me go back to sleep. I don't feel anything here now."

"I had a little something else in mind," said Maharaj, as he touched Mandi's thigh, moved his hand up a little, ready for a bit of sex again.

I watched, mildly interested, as she responded, totally awake, now, ready. Just as he was about to stick it in, I hit him in the balls as hard as I could with my fist. I figured even if I wasn't too effective, strength-wise, he would have to feel that. Immediately, everything drooped. He yelped.

Great! I thought. Now let's see if he'll try to stick a wet noodle up a wildcat's ass!

Smiling, I left the bedroom, leaving the door open so I could hear his wife cursing as he tried unsuccessfully to get his manhood going again.

It was music to my ears. There was no doubt I had made my presence known in this house. No doubt at all!

Gleefully, I turned on the television again and reopened the refrigerator door, then I tormented the dog some more. Neither Maharaj nor his wife got any more sleep that night. I don't know about the boy, since his bedroom door remained closed.

Later, as Maharaj left for work, I found a secluded corner in the guest bedroom where I could rest and think.

I can go after his wife, was my first thought. To my credit, that idea had no attraction for me. I was not interested in "haunting" for the fun of it.

I planned another evening's entertainment for Maharaj when he came home, thinking this might make him receptive to my reaching him in his dreams. He would expect something of the sort, and the whole charade was useless if he did not know who was haunting him and why. I was not after revenge so much as to make him return Jadine's money. For that, I needed a direct confrontation.

I waited.

Maharaj returned home late and had someone with him. He was an older, Indian man, very dark, and wearing a turban and one of those silly wraparound things the pundits and witch doctors usually wore. Dhoti, I think it was called. I always thought the things looked like overgrown diapers.

I moved into the living room to see what transpired. I knew the visitor was there because of me. Probably the cousin. I would have to listen carefully, as they had probably discussed this on their way here. I was very curious as to what this guy thought he might accomplish.

The pundit said, "Are you sure you haven't offended someone? Usually these spirits leave quickly enough if they have no strong reason to bother someone, but the type of activity you mentioned tells me something is extremely interested. I need to know if you offended someone, if that someone is recently dead, or if that someone has access to the spirit world."

"No one that I know of," Maharaj answered, with no hesitation.

Liar! I thought, and turned the television volume up as high as I could.

Immediately, the pundit started chanting and sprinkling water from a lota, and I was forced into one corner of the room. I had to strain to continue listening to the conversation, and I didn't want to miss anything.

I kept pushing and slowly I was able to return. The prayers had had an immediate effect, but it was not permanent. In fact, it was dissipating almost before the echo of the words was over.

"Still here," the pundit said. "Yes, we will have to do something, I think."

In a pig's ass! I thought.

I moved back to a point just behind Maharaj, determined to practice a bit of patience for a change. I did not want to advertise my presence again and miss more of the conversation. These pundits or witch doctors were able to accomplish something on my level, or people would not call on them. I wanted to know what I was up against, for I had unfinished business here.

The pundit told Maharaj, "This spirit is aware of us now. I originally considered forcing it into a bottle and corking it in, but this requires an element of surprise which we do not have. Of course, if you knew the spirit before it became a spirit, and could obtain for me a trifle from the dead body, something trivial like a piece of hair, but of course you say you do not know—"

His voice stumbled to an end, as he looked at Maharaj expectantly. "You see," he continued, finally, "we have to prepare the bottle with the bit of hair or whatever you provide, and some clove to hold the spirit. We then force the spirit in, bind him, or her, with rum, and cork the bottle."

Again the pundit waited.

"Out of the question," said Maharaj. "I would have no way to obtain something like that. You must do something with what you have."

"There is nothing I can do to the spirit, not when it is so distinctly aware and you cannot provide me with a tie to the thing's body to give me control. Mr. Maharaj, I am not skilled in the darker arts of trapping spirits without that control, and I am unable to force a spirit to its own grave to allow me access to the remains. I am not that well versed in Obeah. I know the bottle technique and little else, and you are unable to furnish me what I need for that."

Thank God, I thought. I did not want to run into a heavy dose of Obeah. I had heard enough from Jadine to know it was a real danger to me.

"However," the priest said, "since this spirit seems only to be interested in you, and not your wife and son, I think a simple guard should serve our purpose." He then handed Maharaj a small packet wrapped in cloth. "Wear this at all times," he continued. "It should help."

Maharaj looked worried. "What about the other things, the food spoiling, the dog, the television? Will this guard help there?"

"Yes," was the answer. "As long as you do not remove the guard, you will be perfectly safe."

Maharaj put the guard around his neck. As a test, I reached for his cigarette to put it out. Not only did I not reach it, but I felt dizzy and weak when I tried.

Ridiculous! I thought. It works.

The pundit stood. "I must leave now, Mr. Maharaj. Please let me know if there are any more problems."

"All right, BaBa." Maharaj ushered his visitor out the door. Then, fingering his guard, he proceeded with his usual routine of reading the paper and having a drink. I watched. I did not leave.

I attempted to get past this guard-thing several times, but no luck. I stopped trying.

Still, I did not leave.

CHAPTER FOUR

My chance did not come until three nights later. Maharaj removed the guard before taking his shower, and forgot to replace it, leaving it on the toilet tank lid, near the edge. He went to bed, and I waited, hoping.

The boy came in to use the bathroom. I pushed a glass off the kitchen table, startling the boy, and the guard was accidentally brushed into the toilet, as the flush handle was pushed. I listened to the flush sound, satisfied, and watched the boy head for bed, saying nothing. He knew what the guard was, but was not about to admit flushing it away.

Maharaj had removed the guard before when bathing, and had even forgotten to put it back on once, but I had not been able to touch the thing. The boy had been pure luck.

I waited until Maharaj was deep in sleep, then I moved my face close to his and watched until I saw the movements of his eyelids which meant he was dreaming. I cleared my mind, concentrated on Maharaj, channeled my energy, and tried to push my consciousness into his.

I was in his dream!

I looked around, startled, although this had been my intention from the beginning. Prior to now, I had not been convinced it was even possible. I checked myself and found I looked as I always had. I looked outward, at the dream.

The scenario was simply a well-tended park, and I heard music in the distance. I found Maharaj near the center, near a fountain. He was naked, and three dazzling girls were ministering to him. His head lolled back, his eyes glazed, as the youthful figures used their fingers and mouths on him with enthusiasm and passion. His back was arched, so I knew he doubtless was near orgasm in a wet dream.

The asshole just finished sex in real life! This guy is a real glutton! If he finished what he had started, he would wake up. Can't have that, I thought. Time for a monkey wrench in the works.

I coughed to let him know I was there. It was the quickest thing I could think of, and one look at his face confirmed that speed was needed. He looked up, startled. The three girls disappeared, as did his tumescence. I jumped forward and grabbed him by the neck with one hand. It felt good to get my hands on him, but very quickly I found I was having difficulty controlling myself now that I was finally confronting this guy.

His eyes bulged, and the landscape shifted wildly. He was about to wake up, that was obvious. This was my first time at this dream business, so I could expect mistakes as part of the learning process. I eased my pressure on his throat a little, and he broke free from my grasp.

So be it, I thought. If I lose him, I lose him. I had waited so long for this chance, and I wanted to keep his ass in dreamland for a while. But I also wanted him scared. Scared was more important. I would just have to take my chances.

"Wake up now," I said, "and I'll kill you."

His eyes opened wider as he backed away, his fright plain to see, but the landscape steadied.

Suddenly he was clothed, and his muscles grew larger. I gave him a knee in the nuts. The muscle-building abruptly stopped, and he fell to the ground, writhing in pain.

"What are you?" he asked, gasping, but almost over the pain already.

I looked at him for some time, savoring the moment, but wondering what to do next. I had no plans per se.

"Who are you?" he asked again.

"Just a ghost," I answered.

"What do you want?"

"You!" I said, and made a face.

I was enjoying it. I found the dream world quite malleable, so I started changing the dream into a nightmare, complete with poisonous snakes, spiders and other things. I made sure Maharaj was not killed, for I knew that would certainly wake him.

I played for a short time, then grabbed his head with one oversized hand and forced him to face me. When he continued to avert his gaze, I allowed several spiders to crawl over his face and bite him, until he was frightened enough to look me in the eyes. Of all the things I tossed at him, the spiders had been the only thing that really bothered him.

"No more games," I said. "We have to talk."

I felt just a hint of shame at the fact that I had been enjoying this whole business. After all, my whole intent was to talk, and I had let things degenerate pretty badly for this fun session.

"It's payback time," I said. "Time to get down to business, and you are my business."

"I'm dreaming," he replied. "I'll wake up. You can't touch me once I wake. That's why you warned me not to wake up."

I allowed a big grin to appear on my face. "I've changed my mind, asshole," I said, allowing the grin to widen further. "Now I want you to wake up. Go ahead, try me. Make my day. This dream shit is too tame."

He shuddered. "Why?" he asked.

I relaxed, just a little. Close, but I had gotten away with it.

"Jadine Correy," I said. "I'm sure you remember Mrs. Jadine Correy and the two hundred thousand dollars you stole from her."

"You're her husband?"

"My, my," I said. "He can think. Right on, Chanho old chap, old shithead. I want my wife's money returned."

I poked a finger at his chest, watched it enter as if through air, and tickled his heart muscle. It was the same thing Singh had done to me, so I knew firsthand what the effect would be.

He stared at my finger, horrified.

I chuckled a little. "Would you like me to interfere with this little muscle?" I asked. "It's easy, you know. I have enough power to do it. It's much easier than turning on a television."

I grinned broadly at the panic on his face. "Just one little squeeze," I said. "Not even a hard one."

He turned gray.

I removed the finger, stood back to let him recover. "When you wake up," I continued, "I will stay close to you, close enough to squeeze that little muscle if you try to get some pundit to chase me off. There is no way in hell you can get any help in time to stop me from wiping your ass out of this life. Then I'll kick hell out of your spirit as well." I waited for a minute, watching his reactions as he considered what I had been saying.

Satisfied, I continued. "You are going to prepare the necessary papers to transfer Jadine's money back to her, then you're going to have her meet you at the bank and make the transfer. Understand?"

He nodded, his face pasty white.

I pulled free, and he sat up in bed, grunting in terror. His eyes focused, and he stared around the room then got up and padded to the bathroom, turned on the light, and found no guard. He turned the light off, returned to the bedroom and sat on the bed. I made the bedroom light switch on and off, so he would know I was still there. I did it again, for emphasis.

His eyes widened. He got up again, stumbled to his den, turned on that light, and made out a check payable to Jadine. He filled out a standard release form and used a paper clip to hold the check and release form together. He held them in the air so I could see the amount on the check, and the writing on the form.

I gave the lights a flick so he would know I had seen. He opened the briefcase and placed the check and form inside. He left the den, returned to bed, laid there without sleeping.

Finally, morning came, and he got up and returned to his den. He picked up the phone and dialed a number. I strained to hear. It was not Jadine. It was the pundit, the same one who had come here before.

I pinched Maharaj's tongue, effectively silencing him. I increased the pressure until he replaced the receiver, shuddered, and sat down.

I gave him three or four minutes to calm down once more, then I started turning the light in his study on and off. I also gave his ear lobe a serious pinch, from pure wickedness. He grimaced, then picked up the phone and proceeded to dial.

"Is this Mrs. Correy?" he asked.

I listened carefully. It was Jadine. I relaxed. Maybe this will work, I thought. It better, I'm out of fresh ideas.

"Yes," he was saying. "This is Mr. Maharaj from the bank. We have discovered an error in our transaction of last week and find you should have received an additional two hundred thousand dollars. Could you meet me at the bank when we open this morning?" He listened. "Yes, just ask for me. Thank you."

He hung up and stared at the ceiling. "Satisfied?" he asked.

I was, but I didn't bother to react. He didn't expect an answer.

"Who are you talking to, Chanho?" asked his wife, walking into the den to join him.

"Business, darling," he answered.

"At seven in the morning?" she asked. Her voice indicated she didn't believe him.

"Yes, well, it was something I forgot, and I needed to be certain it was taken care of this morning.

She shrugged and left the room again, obviously irritated. "Suit yourself," she said.

Maharaj took a deep breath then reached for the phone and dialed the pundit's number again.

This time I pinched his tongue for a full forty seconds. He glared at the empty room and, finally, stood and went back to his bathroom to shave and get ready for work. Later, clean and dressed, he returned to his den, picked up his briefcase, and started for the door.

I watched him carefully after that. He tried to take a wrong turn twice, still trying to reach the pundit. The first time I messed up his vision. It was easy; I held my hands over his eyes and channeled my energy to opaque my hands slightly. He still could not see me, but he could not quite see through me, either. The second time irritated me a little, so I hit his steering wheel and almost ran him into an oncoming taxi.

He is not a coward, I thought. I have to give him that.

I followed him inside the bank and stationed myself near his desk. In case he thought I was gone, I made his desk lamp flicker on and off a few times.

His fingers twitched, but he did not make any moves to his phone. His mouth moved in a grimace, so I knew he still had a sore tongue. I grinned tightly, knowing he had given me all the proof I needed that my technique was up to the job at hand.

Jadine came in the bank a few minutes after nine. I was right there when Maharaj had her sign the release and handed her the check. I watched her deposit the check and saw the teller make the necessary adjustments to her account. When I was satisfied the transaction was complete, and that Maharaj could not undo it, I returned to him. He was sitting quite still, making no move to the phone, being docile.

Out of sheer maliciousness, I scattered the papers on his desk to the floor and shorted out his light permanently. He did not react, so that took most of the fun out of tormenting him. I left him and followed Jadine home, home to Diego Martin.

I assumed Maharaj would call the pundit after I left, but I was not concerned. I did not intend to go by his home again in any case.

As far as I was concerned, he was history.

CHAPTER FIVE

The whole affair with Maharaj was exhilarating. I was now confident there were things I could do, that I could make myself known, that I could affect events in the real world. It was much more than I had ever believed possible when I was alive.

What next? I wondered. How does a ghost entertain himself and avoid boredom?

I still didn't want to bug Jadine. I knew that any experimenting on my part would be very disturbing to living people, even to Jadine, despite her seeming to be comfortable with the idea of spirits. Being comfortable with an idea, and confronting that idea head on were two different things entirely.

For now I would watch and wait, and strive to design a rational means of communication. I didn't think there was any hurry.

I watched Jadine for about three weeks as she continued to grieve, mostly at night where she wouldn't disturb the children. I watched the little boy growing inside her; she seemed half aware of him, but not sure. She was too busy grieving.

I watched my other two children. Slowly they tried to adjust to a new life, without me. Everything appeared tranquil. However, life is never quiet for too long, and the present hiatus began to unravel.

First, I overheard Charlie reading Jadine a letter from my oldest daughter from my previous marriage. My son had died, and my younger daughter was still paralyzed from the waist down by the accident back in the States that had, eventually, helped with my dying. Singh did most of it, but my frustrations and heart problem had also helped.

My younger daughter had her baby two months early; it was that or lose the baby. The child was alive and doing well, but my daughter was still in serious condition and still paralyzed. I don't know if she knew I was dead; Elizabeth might not have told her. The news was old news to Jadine, just a progress report on a continuing tragedy, but it was the first time I had heard it, the first time I had been in a position where I could hear it.

I found I wanted to go home to the States to comfort my daughters there, to see my first grandchild, Daniel. It was an impossible dream. Even if I could get there, what could I do? Or rather, I knew what I could not do. It would be like scratching an itch, no more. Still, the desire to go was there and became stronger as time passed.

While I was still preoccupied with what was happening back in the States, the other shoe fell. Jadine became ill. It was subtle at first, but it was not morning sickness. It was debilitating, with a slow loss of strength. She became impatient, screaming at the children, losing interest in her housework.

She finally became aware of the new child within her, and, after a pregnancy test confirmed it, started checking with friends about a possible abortion. I wanted her to have the child, but I was not alive to help take care of it and knew it was not my decision to make.

In any event, with the other changes I observed, the sudden temper fits, the despondency, the weakness, and the many little things so out of character, I became convinced the abortion idea was not really hers. Remembering a few things Jadine had told me, I was certain that someone was practicing Obeah on her. I had not felt Obeah to be a viable part of things when I was alive, but I was having strong second thoughts now that I was dead. Not only that, but I was learning to trust these sudden intuitions.

I thought briefly of Singh but could not convince myself he would have any reason to torment me now. Maharaj then came to mind, as I remembered my recent encounter with him. Revenge is a very potent force, and he may well have decided to get back at me through Jadine.

Maharaj is not the type to take defeat in stride, I realized. He will want revenge, that's sure.

However, I needed proof. If he had done nothing and I got involved with him again, it would be unfair to him and possibly dangerous to me. There was no way I could get forewarning of any special protection he might now have or any traps arranged for me.

I searched the house thoroughly, not sure what I was looking for. I found nothing.

Then I checked under the front steps and found a small cloth bag. I opened it and found a piece of yellow lime, pieces of hair, Jadine's name on a piece of paper, and some other things. It radiated evil vibrations that I could sense, and it took all my strength to replace the contents and move the bag to the road ditch near our house. I found a second bag, under the house near our parking area, and got rid of that as well.

It helped almost at once, but during the next week the first bag was replaced. This time was different. It appeared to have some kind of spell on it, because I could not move it.

By now, my urge to go home to the States was shoved back in my mind. I stormed around the house, trying to get Jadine's attention, but only succeeded in alarming her.

I calmed myself. I took the time to think it out.

I decided to try the dream world, as with Maharaj. I had avoided it thus far, wanting Jadine to adjust to life without me, but circumstances had made it my only recourse. Jadine had to remove this thing, because I could not.

I waited impatiently for her to sleep that night, then even more impatiently for her to dream. Then I slipped into her dream, much more easily than with Maharaj. I immediately found myself face to face with my own image, as I entered directly into a nightmare with a setting at our favorite beach at Maracas.

The scene was lovely, but the action was bad news. Something evil but invisible was attacking and consuming my image, making her sit to one side and watch, paralyzed and not able to move. When she attempted to break free and move, a large, booted foot materialized and kicked her in the stomach, which was grossly inflated in a parody of pregnancy.

Enraged, I used her dream stuff to bury the evil and banish the foot. They did not return, so I calmed down, realizing this had been a true nightmare and not some Obeah thing. I took the place of my own image and ran my hands over her stomach, bringing it back to the slight bulge she actually had.

She watched me, watched as everything came back to normal. "Clark?" she asked. "Is it you, boy? You come back, Clark? You here to visit in my dream and thing?

"Hush. Yes, it's really me."

She beamed, happy as a kid with a new toy. "I know you here," she continued. "I hear you around the house and thing. Why you don' come before? You could, boy. You not know you could? I told you plenty times. You don' remember?"

"I knew," I said, finally managing to get in a word, thrilled at the way this was developing. "I just didn't want to upset you."

"That never an upset for me. Miss you plenty, boy. You can always come here, boy. Need you."

I frowned. "You know what I mean, Jadine. It wasn't that I didn't want to. I was afraid, afraid you'd take it wrong, or just be frightened by me." Without volition I moved closer, sat next to her, wanting to touch her, almost forgetting why I was here. This was nothing like what happened with Maharaj, this time I was welcome.

She brought me back to business. "Listen, boy, something tackling me."

I moved away a little and twisted so I could face her. Talk time. Get reaquainted later.

"I know," I said. "That's why I'm here. When you wake up, under the front steps is a brown bag. Have Krishna get rid of it. I don't want you touching it. Check the whole house, and under the house, and in your car. There could be more of them." I paused, thinking, trying to be sure I covered everything.

"Obeah, Jadine," I continued. These bag things are Obeah, and strong. Be sure to get Krishna on this. Don't try to handle it by yourself."

She nodded, her face serious. Then she grinned slightly. "Now look who talking Obeah," she said.

I grinned back. When alive, I had always put down Obeah, even when I was forced to admit she was usually right on these things. My American background made it hard for me to accept. Now I was dead, such things did not seem impossible any more. Not only that, my death had been engineered by one of these Obeah characters. That is hard to ignore.

"Who the Obeah man, Clark boy? You know? I think you right about this being Obeah, but this funny kind of Obeah. Usually they not so easy when they hit. With Obeah, they use big stick. This more like amateur night, so something still hidden from we. Somebody playing with we, boy. Obeah, sure enough, but not right. Who doing this to me? Who this Obeah man, Clark?"

I tried to give a name, couldn't.

"Who the man, Clark?" she insisted, pulling on my arm a little. She watched my face intently, waited.

I tried to tell her about Maharaj but couldn't. Then I tried to talk about Singh and, again, was stymied. She kept watching me and did not seem surprised at my sudden problem. It was something she had been expecting.

"You know," she said. "You know and not able to say. Right?"

I grimaced, ground my teeth in frustration. "Yeah," I answered. "I can't tell you who. It's more than just these bag things, Jadine. This also has to do with how I died, and involves several people still alive. I'll do what I can, or what I'm allowed to do."

She moved closer. "We talk later," she said. "I maybe know enough. How many enemies we got, hey, boy? The bank fellow no like me. This Mr. Singh no like you. That's about it, no biggie. You can' say, but it don' make no never mind."

She moved closer, sending the signal she was tired of the subject at hand. Becoming aware of her closeness, as she had intended, and despite this being a dream, I reached for her and was startled at the warm softness as she accepted my embrace eagerly.

Our clothes disappeared, and I took her there in that dream world. Later we lay on the deserted beach in each other's arms, and I talked. I found I still could not communicate concerning Maharaj or Singh, but I could wear her ear out over her and the children and the new baby.

"I really want it, Clark, boy," she said. "That baby the last thing you give me. But listen, boy, Clark, sometimes I fed up and thing and don' know what to do."

"It's the Obeah making you do this," I said, "and it's a boy."

"A boy," she said, smiling. "I would love another boy. I hope he look like you." Then, "How you really feel, boy? Being dead, I mean."

"Different," I answered, "but I'm not sure what happens next. I sure as hell wasn't ready, and it has not been what I expected."

Understatement of the century, I thought. I never thought too much about life after death, but my few memories did not include any ordinary, everyday scenarios like this.

"How you manage to stay, boy? You never listen to me, so how you know you can?"

I shrugged. I had wondered the same thing. "I guess I listened more than I knew," I said. "When I died, at first I didn't know what had happened, then I didn't want to leave you. I could have, but I had the feeling you might need me, even dead. I didn't know I could stay until I decided to stay. Now maybe you *really* don't need me again. You have your money settled, and now you can settle this Obeah thing, with Krishna's help. What do you think?"

"I think you talk silly and stupid," she said. "Course I need you here. You think I want to lose you when I just got you back?"

She paused, then continued in a firmer voice, rising to her feet and pacing a nervous circle. "Also you being a dumbhead. Maybe Obeah, and maybe not, And maybe Krishna get through, and maybe not. But this not settled yet. If it keep coming back, it could be dangerous and thing, Clark, boy. You have to stay with me a while, boy. I need you here. I scared like hell, boy. You can stay after things settled too, then I know you always here with me."

She still paced. She knew how nervous it made me, but knowing had never stopped her when I was alive. And it wasn't stopping her now. Finally, a little irritated, I grasped her arm and pulled her back down with me.

"You can't even see me," I protested, "except like now, in a dream, and you'll never be certain I came back. Not for sure."

"Yes I will," she snapped. "When we find Obeah thing. Then I know for real. That be proof. Besides, Clark, boy, dream better than nothing, boy. Lot better than nothing."

I stared at the Maracas beach in her dream world. It looked real, as real as the one I remembered. Jadine's memory was awesome. I thought about what she had said, that she wanted me to stick around. Too many memories, I wondered. She wants something to take the edge off some of those memories. With me here, she can start living again, she can avoid living in her memories.

"Maybe better than zero," I answered, finally. "I can't make you happy, though, not like this. I'm just too damned limited."

Seeing my frustration, she moved closer in our embrace. Not a good scene, I thought. Time to change the subject.

"Listen Jadine," I said. "Please get Elizabeth on the phone and find out what's going on. Will you do that?"

"Yes, I will. You know, then?"

I felt the tears in my eyes, brushed them away. I had wanted to change the subject, but I had picked a rough one. I hadn't known how strongly I felt until the question was out. Oh, well, I thought. I can get this thing in the open now, I can find out.

"I heard Charlie read you the letter," I mumbled, still preoccupied. I looked down the beach, and saw the grove of coconut trees where we had gone so often for beach parties. I looked the other direction, where the fishing village was located. I saw the waves, the long stretch of clean sand, the beautiful water.

Jadine?" I asked. "Is there any way I can go there and see the baby. After we're sure this business about the Obeah bags is ended, I mean. I don't want to leave here for long, but I want to see my grandchild."

Her face radiated her uncertainty. "I not sure, boy. I always hear spirit not allowed to cross water and thing. I will ask Krishna."

The landscape wavered, the beach seemed to fall in on itself. I tried to get to my feet, alarmed.

"Clark, boy," she cried. "I waking up."

"Not yet," I answered. "Not yet. Please. Not yet."

It was too late. She was awake, and I was ejected. She opened her eyes slowly and whispered, "Clark?" She could not see me, but she sensed me.

She cried silently, lay quiet a few more minutes, then sat up and put on a robe. She drank a cup of tea in the kitchen, trying to settle her nerves, thinking about her dream. Finally, she returned to bed, to toss and turn and lie sleepless until morning.

When she got up, she called Krishna. He arrived in about a half hour. She told him what was going on and let him take over.

I followed the two of them as they searched and watched Krishna find two Obeah bags. He continued looking, not missing any place, even checking through the car. Finally he left, taking the bags with him.

I wondered what to do next I was sure Maharaj was not after her. It was me he wanted, and Jadine was just his tool to reach me. It had to be connected with Maharaj. I could not see any other option. I had thought briefly of Singh, trying to be thorough, but rejected the notion. There seemed no reason for him to be involved. No, I thought, it's Maharaj, and it's a trap. Has to be.

Over the next few months, Jadine's belly swelled enough to be noticeable. At my urging, and following my directions, she transferred her account to a different bank. It was not an easy task, because the money was in trust, but my will had left provisions allowing for the transfer.

During those months, there were three more Obeah bag incidents, one of them in the car, together with two eggs, colored pink and black. There also was a scary incident where something evil invaded the house and humbugged the children. I stormed around the house, in a panic, and it left. No credit to me, but at least the house was free again. Krishna was a very frequent visitor, and extremely helpful. I was very worried by this continued persistence.

As the time passed, I was learning about what I could do and could not do. I thought that in a showdown I might be able to show Maharaj how nasty Americans could be.

As I gained strength and knowledge, it was Jadine who held me back. I had started feeling I could handle anything some silly witch doctor or pundit could dream up, but she was afraid of the power of Obeah over spiritual things, and I was wholly spiritual.

We went into her sixth month of pregnancy with matters still unresolved. I wanted to go after the source of the problem, but she held me off. She warned me Obeah was much more than the little tame things we had encountered.

I still was unable to tell Jadine about Maharaj or Singh. I found myself avoiding any mention of anything that concerned either of them. For that reason alone, I listened to Jadine. I knew Singh was Obeah, and I suspected Maharaj of hiring someone in Obeah to torment Jadine. My worst fear came on me gradually. What if Maharaj hired Singh.

Time passed. Then, one morning, something evil pushed Jadine from the top of the stairs. I saw a shimmering in the air and tried to warn her, but I was still unable to get through to her except in dreams, or through little things like light switches. The evil left at my approach, but Jadine lay still as death at the bottom of the stairs.

Frantic, I managed to get the phone moved from the next room to a point near her body, then entered her as a dream, hoping she would be there. I was lucky.

I wandered through the dreamscape and finally found her curled in a ball near the beach scene. "Jadine!" I exclaimed, rushing to her.

She raised her head. "Clark? Please, Clark, help me. My belly hurt bad."

"Jadine, I can't do anything. You have to bring yourself awake and use the telephone. Call for help."

Slowly she sat up and looked at me. The dream faded, and I watched her dial a number. I assumed it was the ambulance, for I had written that number on a label on the phone before I had died. For emergencies.

Afterwards, the phone fell from her limp fingers, and she lapsed into unconsciousness again. After long, anxious minutes, the ambulance arrived and the attendants got her loaded.

I stayed with her on the trip to the hospital, through the doctor visits and everything. I stayed until I heard a doctor say she would be okay and that the baby had not been harmed.

Then, my rage like a cloud around me, I left.

CHAPTER SIX

I went straight to Maharaj's home though I knew he would be at work. But his wife was home, and I could make her bring him to me. I was not in a mood to accept any delay. I wanted Maharaj, and I wanted him now. I felt a strength I never had before, and I knew my rage was the cause, the source of the strength. Knowing I would need that strength, I nursed my rage, fed on it.

The door was not locked. I entered and went on a rampage, knocking over lamps, breaking mirrors, flicking the lights, turning on the stereo, spoiling the dinner that was still cooking, tormenting the dog, and even managing to start some flooding in the bathroom. Maharaj's wife was thoroughly frightened and called her husband at once.

Hearing the panic in her voice, I was almost ashamed, but then I remembered Jadine in the hospital. All shame was burned to nothing. I reached out and started playing with her hair, getting her more frantic than ever, and resulting in fresh screams while she was still on the phone.

Satisfied, I went to the front curb and walked quickly up the street, leaving Mandi's screams behind. I had no more horrors for the wife.

Maharaj sped home, and I intercepted him several blocks up the street.

He was not alone. There were two men in the back seat.

I looked closer and realized they were not men, or not real men.

Must be Obeah, I thought. Not only that, but I recognized them. They had been at the cemetery when I was getting buried, standing next to some Indian guy. Maharaj hadn't known me or Jadine then, so these two must be from Singh. Maharaj had brought in some professional help, and these two uglies were the result.

Maharaj was ready for me. It all had been a trap to get me here. I studied the two briefly and knew they were no more alive than me. I could sense it. They were not associates of Singh. They had to be his tools, and they were here to do a job for him.

I shuddered at my conclusions. I had stopped worrying about Singh as I assumed I was out of his reach when I died. This was premature on my part, because these two were definitely dead, and they were connected somehow with Singh, or controlled by him. Maharaj may have started this, but he was no longer acting alone.

The car was still moving, but to my heightened senses it seemed to be barely moving as I tried to cope with what I was learning. I walked alongside, peering through the side window, to see the two spirits more clearly.

One of the men, definitely negro, had a face that looked like it had been half eaten away by worms and eyes like a feral cat. He was wearing his hair in the Rasta style, that peculiar hair style which made the hair look like coils of dirty rope hanging haphazardly, the style the Trinidadians called "dredd". It was a style for long hair, which was plaited in loose, heavy coils three quarters of an inch in diameter or so and, according to Trinidadians, never again washed. It was not a pretty style, but seemed to go very well with the half-eaten face.

The other man had an ugly, half-festered wound on the side of his head, but I could not decide if he were negro or Indian. I thought he might be that mixture the natives called "Dogler". The wound looked as if it had been dealt by an animal, as I could see claw or tooth marks.

I had finally seen something dead like me, and the somethings I saw were evil. I felt the evil as if it were a physical force.

My anger rekindled as I studied the car's occupants. The fact that I was dealing with Singh again scared the shit out of me, even if it were his two spiritual tools rather than him personally. He had handled me from a distance before I died, using the dog thing. Now he was handling me from a distance again, using these two spirit things.

I had been free of him. I had to die to do it, but I thought he had not been interested after. Then this Maharaj asshole brought him back in the picture, and, now, Jadine was the focus of the thing.

So Maharaj was still my first concern. He hired Singh, so these things had to do what Singh wanted, but it was Maharaj that had set things in motion, so he was the one responsible.

My timeless hiatus was past. It was time for action. I wrapped my rage around me, as if it were an invisibility cloak, and entered the car carefully while it was still moving, trying to keep the two things from seeing me.

I'm not sure why I thought they couldn't see me; it was a ridiculous notion on the face of it, and later events proved it to be a ridiculous notion in all ways. I doubt I could have gotten in that car unseen under any conditions. They wanted me in and, most likely, helped me. They wanted me to do what I could so they could see what my strengths were.

Maharaj had expected me to do something, the spirits with him expected me to do something, and I had come here to do something.

So I did the something!

I grabbed the steering wheel and yanked with all my strength. The big car careened to the side, smashed into a row of parked cars, and threw Maharaj against the front edge of his side window, opening a nasty gash on his forehead.

"Oh God!" he screamed. "He's here."

Then I held his tongue, twisting and pulling, pinching and ripping at it, silencing him. I could see blood in his mouth, so I knew the tongue was in deep trouble. I wanted to get busy on him, but some inner alarm kicked in.

I had been in the car far too long.

I did not hesitate. I was already moving as I felt the two spirits reaching for me. I just managed to elude them as I left the car. I think I surprised them. They did not expect me to just cut and run.

Maharaj managed to open his door and stagger out, starting for the concrete walk to his house. I sidestepped away from the guy with the wormholes and tripped Maharaj, then I had to duck around the bashed-head character to reach him again. This time I jammed my finger in his ear, hard, and laughed grimly to myself as he screamed.

The other two were on me then, but my rage still fueled me. I managed to tear free. Maharaj had almost reached his door when I tripped him again and watched him butt into the door with his head as he fell. The sound made me grin, it was the sound of full involvement between head and door. He stood, staggered a little, and walked right through old Wormholes.

That confirmed he could not see his guards, and probably didn't know they were here. That might explain why they let me fix him up. They could be providing some protection, but Maharaj was not in charge of things. If they actually wanted me, protection for Maharaj was purely coincidental. I did not plan to let them have me, and I was not going to allow Maharaj to escape from me.

I had no way of knowing how much power they had, but I saw them and felt them, so I had to assume they were as real to me as live people were when I was alive. That meant I was outnumbered at least.

Also, I had to wonder if this Obeah gave them any advantages. Normal common sense dictated I should get away while I could, but I was still pissed off and determined to hurt Maharaj.

He stood and again moved to his door. After you, I thought, and kicked him in the balls, knocking him into the door again.

"Mandi!" screamed Maharaj. "Mandi, let me in."

No answer. Maharaj slipped to the side of the house and soon was at the back door. I eluded my two pursuers again and tripped Maharaj before he could enter the house. He stood again and squeezed past the door. I joined him and slammed the door on the other two spirits, hoping Maharaj had another protection guard going. It might not hold my unsavory friends long, but every little bit helps.

While the others noisily worked on the door, trying to get past the guard I had hoped was there, I again turned my attention to Maharaj.

He tried to go up the stairs, but those bangs on the head had him half blinded, and he ended up crawling. He still cried for his wife, and I heard her answer from outside and knew she was coming. He reached the top of the stairs and stood up, and I shattered a mirror located there, sending several fragments into his face. Then I closed the bedroom door at the last minute, so he ran into it and almost bounced back down the stairs.

I heard the back door open, and then Mandi screamed downstairs. I knew the other two had slipped in with her, and I was in trouble. Mandi continued to squeal downstairs, heavy screams this time. I grinned a little, knowing the two uglies had paused to torment her more than a little.

I started throwing things at Maharaj from the bathroom, razors, cups, soap, trying to force him back to the edge of the stairs, wanting him to fall as Jadine had fallen. As he neared the edge, I saw my opening and pushed. With a hoarse cry, he slipped, his arms windmilling, and he tumbled to the bottom, landing in a disorganized heap. He immediately got up, limping, and started up the steps again. By then the two uglies were converging on me, big grins on their faces.

I had overplayed it by dropping Maharaj down the stairs, because, now, I had their full attention As long as I had tormented Maharaj upstairs, they had been satisfied to wait, amusing themselves with Mandi. When Maharaj hit the bottom of the steps they could no longer amuse themselves. The commotion broke their concentration on fun and brought them back to business. I was that business.

As they neared, I felt a strong lethargy creeping over me. Either they had some power I did not, or the impetus furnished to me by my rage was waning. Whatever the cause, I knew I had to get out quickly. I could not resist one last ripping squeeze on Maharaj's tongue, and then I fled for the open back door, the two avenging spirits right behind me.

As I left, I assumed that all I had to do was to make tracks and get the hell out and that would be that. My smug thoughts on my future safety quickly evaporated as I saw I could not seem to shake my pursuers. It was not to be that easy. I ran, and they followed. They were not tied to Maharaj. They did not have to stay behind as I fled.

Once they had me in sight, they appeared to be attached to me. I hurried down the street toward the Diego Martin Main Road, away from St. James, following a desperate idea, a possible sanctuary, and they stayed with me. The weakness I felt earlier was stronger, and my idea of sanctuary began to feel flimsy. I had nothing else.

They were relentless, and nothing seemed to shake them off. Singh, I thought. It was not just a job to get rid of an unwanted spirit for a client. He wants me.

Slowly, steadily, I grew weaker. I wrestled with my mind, trying to think of another way out. No good. I had to make the sanctuary idea work, and sanctuary was St. Mary's, the Catholic church.

The church appeared to my right, and I entered, disturbing the flames on candles as I came in. Something tried to eject me. I stayed, my fear empowering me.

The two spirits could not enter.

They raged outside for hours, finally gave up, and left. I knew when they were gone; I knew from some place deep inside without having to look.

Shaken to my core, I emerged from the church. I knew I could not re-enter. Only my desperate need had allowed me entry in the first place. I came out and slowly confirmed my pursuers were gone. I started down the street again, more tired than I ever was in life.

Slowly I moved to the hospital and found Jadine's room, where she was asleep and dreaming. Wearily, I managed to enter her consciousness.

"Jadine?" I called, as I searched among the jungle landscape of her dream. It looked like the rain forest in the Oropuche area. I had built a raw water line there.

"Clark? Hey, boy, what wrong?" Her voice seemed to come from above the trees, to my right. I changed direction a little. "You look so tired," she continued, "like you beat up ten times."

"I just had a session with two Obeah things," I answered. "At least, I think they were Obeah."

"Oh, no." She was with me now, by my side on a well-kept path that had just emerged. Her face radiated her concern.

"Yeah," I continued. "I might have scared their boss enough to leave you alone. I think it's all over. You can relax now."

"Then tell me he name," she said, watching me closely. She could see how tired I was, how I drooped. She knew it was my encounter that had caused this. We knew each other so well, We didn't have to ask some things. We had reached the point, before I died, where we seemed to read each other's minds.

I could not answer her question.

Her face changed. Mild concern had been replaced with a touch of fear, fear for me.

"You still not allowed to say name and thing," she said. "Obeah still in the mix." Her voice softened. "If it over for you, you could tell me he name. So it not over. Obeah still after you. You do know name, don' you?"

"Yes," I answered.

"I don' mean name of person you vex with. I can guess that easy, has to be connect with my money suddenly a lot more. That one, he got to be the ugly bank fellow. But he not Obeah. No way. You hit Obeah thing for sure, so I no care about bank man name. I after name of Obeah man."

We had stopped by now. She was standing with her hands on her hips, tears glistening in her eyes. "Singh?" she asked. "You had he real vex and he Obeah. Or did bank fellow get someone new?"

I looked at her, surprised. She had figured out my whole situation. I still could not say Maharaj's name, or Singh's name. I felt sure Maharaj had hired Singh, but I couldn't tell Jadine what I thought.

"I'm having problems with my answer," I said. "I can't spit a name out. Why do you think the bank guy isn't involved anymore? That is what you're getting at, isn't it?"

"Clark, boy, you same as say bank guy's name already. Can' even do that if he heavy in the thing. And you not listen good. You got the real thing going now. Obeah man, he show he claws a little bit. Bank fellow no have claws. And, boy, something interested in you, that sure."

I thought about it, something after me for myself. It seemed to make sense. "Maharaj," I said, the ties on my tongue suddenly free.

"Oh, Clark." She took me in her arms. "Clark, boy, you must be more careful. That prove bank fellow he not the problem. Stay away from he though, 'cause Obeah man maybe left guard with he."

"So what can I do about it?"

"Don' know," she answered. "Hope it not Singh," she continued. "He a real nasty man. He really in deep with spirits and them. Word is he kill plenty people just for fun and business and thing. Real nasty."

We sat on a patch of soft grass, near the path. I shivered a little and felt a sudden chill through my body. And that's the guy I chose to insult, I thought. Probably wouldn't have made any difference if I had known, though. Singh had stepped on my temper, and I wasn't too reasonable when that happened, even after dying. Even if it appeared he hadn't wanted me dead so quickly. Sooner or later he would have taken me out. Jadine noticed my sudden shiver, hugged me close. We clung together.

Then she tightened her embrace, adding a few touches I remembered from when I was alive.

I responded.

CHAPTER SEVEN

Jadine had her baby in late January of 1981. It was a little boy as I had told her, Nickolas. There were no additional problems. I observed Maharaj for a while but there was no sign of Wormface or Bashed Head. He was wearing a hearing aid now and had some difficulty in talking but, otherwise, was unchanged.

Jadine's fears that I should be agonizing about Singh, or whoever helped Maharaj, were fading as time passed. I still couldn't say Singh's name, but nothing appeared interested in me any more, either. It was the old trap; nothing had happened, so nothing would.

I did not go near Singh's office to check him out. I had enough sense to avoid any contact there. If it were him, maybe he was dropping it. It seemed a reasonable hope.

I initiated experiments to see how far I could travel, if there were limitations, if I could go wherever I wanted as when I were alive. My beginning trials were for Trinidad, itself, and I found I could go anywhere I wanted within the confines of the island.

Then I tried Tobago, the sister island, but could not walk or swim or go by boat. Finally, I was able to get there by traveling with Jadine in a plane, but I could visit only two days before I snapped back.

I did get there, though. With that thought, I convinced Jadine to buy a plane ticket to the States, so I could check it out. If I were able to cross over the ocean with her and still be limited to that same two days, that would be enough time to see my grandson, Daniel. Of course, if the distance were important I would not make it. Instead, I would be zapped back to my grave as happened with Tobago.

She managed the tickets for mid-March, after Carnival, and after Nickolas was old enough to travel. If I were yanked back, Jadine could still visit my family, take pictures and vacation a little.

When mid-March rolled around, we were on our way. I was extremely uncomfortable from the moment we took off. The discomfort grew as the plane continued on its way, and as we reached the halfway point I felt I was about to be pulled off the plane.

I had anchored myself to Jadine's dream world early on, and this helped a great deal. But the kids were so restless, especially the baby, that Jadine was only dozing off for short periods. Luckily, little Jamie, almost five now, got bored enough to fall asleep, and I was able to enter his dream world. It was not much, but it allowed me to hold on, to stay with my family.

Soon, water or no water, the plane landed in New York City at Kennedy Airport. I was just a short step away from New Jersey, and I had an outside chance of seeing Daniel, my grandson.

Jadine stepped off the plane and moved through customs, then went through the hassle of boarding a helicopter for the short trip to Newark Airport. Elizabeth was to meet her and the kids at Newark. I was amazed all over again at Jadine's patience. She had the baby in her arms and Karen and Jamie holding to her side, crying to be carried. She did not scream or yell. She managed.

After the brief helicopter journey, Jadine walked to the main concourse to wait, for she was early. Somehow she was able to get the kids settled a little on the lobby chairs. They fell asleep almost at once.

Elizabeth arrived. I stared at her. I really had thought I would never see her again. I watched as she and Jadine embraced, a little awkwardly because Elizabeth never had completely accepted her as a member of the family. I followed as they moved through the crowded concourse and the parking lot to Elizabeth's car. The kids caused a few problems, but there were two to handle things now.

By this time I was having difficulty keeping up. The extreme discomfort I had felt since losing Jamie's dream world as an anchor was getting worse. I found myself shuffling and tripping over my own feet. My vision was blurring, and I found it hard to concentrate on what was happening around me.

I held desperately to my tenuous ties with Jadine, very frightened now. As the pressure tugging at me mounted, I worried about what would happen when I snapped back from this great distance. It was a bit late to do anything about it, but knowing that did not ease the pressure and did not lessen my fear.

I was on the verge of losing my battle, but I was still determined to see my grandson and my injured daughter. I focused on my determination, used that.

Slowly Elizabeth moved the big Buick into the traffic, heading for Route One South to Metuchin, where she lived with Jerry her husband, Carrie, and Daniel. They had taken on that burden with no complaint, and I would be forever grateful for that.

It was night, and Elizabeth drove fast once free of the city traffic. The conversation lapsed and Jadine dozed, allowing me a small respite from the mounting strain as I held to her dream world, fighting to stay with her.

"I don't think I'll make it," I told her dream image. "I'm being pulled apart."

I looked at myself, saw my body fading and losing shape. The signs of my struggle were actually visible. The strain was terrible.

"Try," she answered. "We almost there, boy. Not far now."

"It's only your dreams holding me," I answered. "You and Jamie. Try to see the baby quickly, Jadine. I must see Daniel. That's why we're here."

I was frantic now. My image wavered. I was losing control. So long a trip, so long a fight. I was so afraid it was for nothing. "Help me," I cried out.

"I try," Jadine answered, "but what happens when you have to leave and thing? How I know?"

I shrugged. I had no idea how to answer that question. "I don't know," I answered, finally. "I guess I'll just go back and be waiting for you at home."

"Promise?" she murmured. "You have to promise that you wait."

"Absolutely," I said, not at all sure I would be able to keep the promise but knowing I would try.

"We're home," Elizabeth announced, and Jadine woke. Sleepy heads looked up from the back seat. The baby started crying.

Desperately, I held to Jadine as she went into the house. There was nothing more she could do. The kids were wide awake and testing her patience to the limit. I would have to hang on however I could.

"You'll want to see the baby," Elizabeth said when the kids and suitcases were unloaded, and we were inside.

"Yes," Jadine replied. "I want to see Daniel. I want to see he now."

I caught a brief glimpse of Daniel. Then I was snapped away into nothingness.

*   *   *

I had no idea how much time had elapsed, but I came to my senses aware I was at the Western Cemetery in St. James. I had survived, but I was very weak.

I did not move right away, nursing that glimpse of Daniel, aware that it might be the only one I would ever get. I thought of Jadine, wondering if she had returned from the States yet. Since I did not know how long it had been since my forced return, I did not know if she were back or still with my daughter.

I continued to lie motionless, gathering my strength. I was not in my coffin. I was lying on the ground, on top of my grave.

I suspect the nearness to my dead body, my corpse, had triggered me not to stay too close even before my awareness had returned. It was too strong a reminder of what my status was.

Finally I looked around me, curious as to my surroundings, wondering if this place were as benign as it seemed. Of course, where else could I go?

This place felt close to being home, since my body rested here. Benign or evil, this was now my place. At least it was mine if I wanted it.

I thought about that and quickly decided I did not want it, not yet. I was not yet through with the world of the living, and I still had some unfinished business.

Jadine, I thought. Time to check her out. It was night, so I should catch her asleep if she were back. I could visit.

CHAPTER EIGHT

Wormface and Bashed Head caught me as I passed through the main gate of the cemetery, and I had no idea they were there. They were accompanied by a large, brown dog with red eyes, and I knew at once that the dog was the one from my dreams before I died, the one that had helped me die, Singh's dog. This dog had never been alive. I knew that now. I was not sure if he were dead, but I knew he was not alive.

I tried to break away, but my efforts were useless. The dog grinned at me, his eyes like whirlpools of pure evil. I went with them, no choice.

I found myself staring at the dog. As I stared, his color changed to black. I blinked, the color faded, returned as brown.

Slowly, I began to comprehend that the only thing certain was the uncertainty. The color was brown, then it seemed black. The size appeared to alter from moment to moment; the shape itself, the "dog" look, seemed to be variable, somehow. The worst were the eyes, the whirlpool look, the spinning effect, although I was confident they hadn't moved.

My weak attempts to escape melted to nothing under that steady gaze, and I felt myself walking by the cemetery wall between my two captors.

A young boy stiffened as we approached and crossed the road, running. I did not know what he saw or sensed, but he was aware of something. Being a Trinidadian, he did not intend to stick around.

"Ought to tackle he," said Wormface.

Surprised, I looked at him, took in the dirty, ropelike braids of his hair, the ravaged face, the sudden gleam of interest in the intense eyes.

I guess I shouldn't have been surprised. After all, I could talk. With no one to talk to except Jadine in her dreams, I did not bother much with it.

"No, man," said the other. "You know we chained to handle this man. Besides, Fido wouldn't like it."

The dog grinned again, understanding every word being spoken. Intelligence was obvious. That, alone, was enough to blow my mind

Not a dog, I thought. Whatever else this thing might be, it is not a dog. No way.

I kept trying to get away, but somehow they had me tied to them. I could not get free, and I had no control over my movements at all. I went where they wanted me to go, and I would find out where I was going when I got there.

We moved down the street, taking our time. It was full dark.

A taxi moved by slowly, looking for fares but not having much luck. My captors moved into the back seat of the car, carrying me along somehow. The dog followed.

My mind reeled.

The driver went rigid behind the wheel and stared at his empty back seat. His eyes went wider. He pulled over to the curb, jumped out, and ran, leaving his taxi where it was. He had taken his keys from the car, but nothing else. He ran like the devil himself was after him.

"Oh, well," said Bashed Head. "Worth a try. So we have to walk. Don' guess that going to kill we." He giggled.

His companion grinned.

The dog grinned.

"Where are you taking me?" I asked. "And why?"

"Down by the old American base, in Chaguaramas," replied Wormface. "Someone want to put a leash on you."

"Better not try to run," added Bashed Head. "Fido here he fix you up."

I dropped the conversation for the moment, trying to think things through. I should have known Singh would not just give up. My jaunt to the States gave him his chance. He knew I would be forced back, that I would be weak and easily captured, so he just waited.

I still might have broken and run, taking my chances, but this dog thing was an unknown factor. I had to find out more.

These two characters were in awe or fear of the animal or whatever it was, so there was a danger here. I studied my two unwelcome companions.

"Are you working for Singh?" I asked, finally.

Wormface giggled. "You could say so."

His friend laughed, low, almost a growl. "Owned is better word," he said.

"Why?" I asked. "You should be free like me."

I waited for an answer, wondering how spirits could be controlled by anything. How could a spirit be anything but free.

Bashed Head looked at me. "Like you now," he said. "Not like you later."

"Nothing 'gainst you," Wormface said, "but we not free, no way, and now we have to bring you to the man that own we." He indicated the beast. "He own Fido, too."

I still couldn't see how they could be restrained if they decided to do their own thing. How the hell could they be forced.

"What if I just walk away?" I asked, curious. They had taken off the spell controlling my walking back in the Cocorite area, and had told me about it. They didn't feel they needed it any more, I guess. I continued to walk with them, knowing that if I didn't they'd just use the spell again. I preferred walking on my own.

"You walk off," said Bashed Head, "and Fido stop you. Don' need spell again. Spell and them, they no last long. Fido, though, he last forever. When he through, we still take you in, slightly damaged. The damage stay with you forever." He lifted a mangled arm for me to see. "I try running couple times. He faster than we, and strong. You see my arm. Not pretty. Have to think real hard before I try again."

He use Fido to punish we, too," added Wormface. "That done dry, no heat, no torture, no bad horrors, just hurt we and drop it. But we run, and he turn loose for real. Fido real bad, he."

"I don't believe it," I said.

Wormface giggled. It was not a fun sound. "Who care?" he asked. "Go ahead and try. Make me no never mind. Fido he no hassle me, not this job. Go ahead. I no watch he in action for a while. Roy been goody-goody lately and maybe Fido out of practice and thing. Maybe you make it."

We all stopped, and they looked at me expectantly, waiting. The dog watched me, his eyes almost hypnotic.

I shrugged. "Not now."

I turned to Wormface. "Your friend's name is Roy. Do you have a name too? Or should I just call you Wormface?"

"Screw you," he growled.

"He Malcolm," grinned Roy. "He no like he name. I guess he don' like Wormface even more."

Malcolm glared at Roy, who grinned back. We continued along the Carenage Main Road, past the Diego Martin turnoff. I was glad for the names. I was getting tired of thinking in terms of their appearance. Names made them seem less terrible somehow. I might need these two some day, unlikely as that seemed now.

Roy, the one I had been calling Bashed Head, tired of baiting Malcolm, turned to me. "Maybe you should run," he said. "I hear one man make it once. He not even damage too bad. Course, that years ago. Nobody make it recent."

Malcolm grinned. "Yeah, he no damage bad. Make people sick look at he, but don' make they faint."

"Truth," came Roy's answer. "But he no need to be pretty. He dead."

I shivered, the fear strong in me, but I continued walking. There wasn't much to see along this stretch of road. Lots of homes, but none of the fancy ones. There were not too many people on the road. So I walked, for there seemed to be no other choice. Meanwhile, these two appeared willing to talk, so perhaps I could learn something useful.

Roy spoke up again. "I was murdered," he said. "I get caught when I try to humbug my murderer. The Obeah man, Mr. Singh, he waiting for me. He say he like murdered spirits. They more strong. People all goody-goody in real life all weak when they dead. If you murdered and thing, that leave you with strength, and then you be more useful to he."

Singh, I thought. I was right. It was Singh. First he kills me, and now he still wants to control me after I'm dead.

"Maybe if we all worked together, we could get free," I ventured.

Roy looked like he was considering it. "No," he said, finally. "Not enough, just we. Maybe with someone else, but not with Mr. Singh. He too strong, man. He got he pets, and he always guarded."

I was getting more worried as the discussion continued. What bothered me most was the fear and respect they had for Singh, a little shit of a man who had not impressed me worth a damn. These two characters, rough and nasty, were completely under his spell for some reason. The respect appeared to have been instilled by fear, but what could this clown do to cause such fear.

"That dog real bad, too," added Malcolm. "He got more than teeth and claws. He pure Obeah." He looked at me and grinned. "That dog never live. He born by Obeah, and live on humbugging. If Mr. Singh die, Fido die, so he very loyal to Mr. Singh."

I thought about what they had said. It appeared this Fido was the main thing they feared. I looked at him. He just grinned back at me, with that stupid, doggy grin.

"Who make you all vex and thing?" asked Roy. "That bank fellow?"

I was glad for the interruption to my little side thing with the dog. "Yeah," I answered. "I was pissed off at the bank fellow."

"He maybe sorry one day," continued Roy. "Sometimes Mr. Singh he give we a little free time, and you can go visit he then. Mr. Singh he give you power, too."

"I think I did everything to him I wanted to do," I said. "I don't need to see him again."

Roy had a disbelieving smirk on his face. Malcolm just shrugged.

Mistake, I thought. They won't tell me anything useful if I seem completely different from them. I will have to be more flexible.

We moved on in silence for a while

"He let me have my murderer," said Roy, finally. "Three years after he catch me, Mr. Singh turn me loose on he, reward and thing." He grinned. "Fix he up good. He die slow."

He turned then and asked Malcolm, "Ain't that right?"

"Yeah, you fixed me," was the answer. "So shut up. We both in same place now."

Roy laughed. "He still a client when Mr. Singh let me have he. That show how loyal Mr. Singh be to he clients."

He smirked, Malcolm scowled. I listened, satisfied to let them ramble on. Maybe I could get something useful. They didn't seem to be restricting what they talked about, they just said whatever popped into their minds.

I watched the changing scenery as we continued, what I could see of it in the intermittent moonlight. As we walked, the population seemed to dwindle. Most of this road was along the coast, but it was not a beach-type coast. Where every valley and hillside had been packed with homes and small businesses, now the roadside was bare for long stretches.

"We get along good now," Roy continued. "Mr. Singh he use we as a team. Sometimes we get Fido, sometimes not. You, you get away from we once and hurt a client. So Mr. Singh, he wonder why you special, why you get strong so quick. Usually he wait longer to collect a new dead. He picky 'bout who he kill for staff and thing, and he want they to get strong on they own. But you too fast, so you he want bad. That why Fido come with we, just to be sure you no get loose again, and to make it quick."

He paused and I waited, but he didn't say anything else. If I had wanted to be positive Singh had killed me or had me killed, here it was. Surely he couldn't expect any kind of cooperation after this.

So I had a few answers. I had wondered how Singh could have control over spirits, but this dog thing provided at least one answer; an evil force that could damage even spiritual flesh, something that could mutilate even if it did not kill. We could not die twice, but the mutilation threat was very potent.

Still to be answered were the questions of what that Fido thing was, whether it was unique, whether it could be manipulated, whether Singh had a way of seeing his leashed spirits and his little pet, and whether he could be dealt with in some way; and most important to me, whether his leashed spirits could be circumvented. I still had the mistaken impression that the talkative spirits with me somehow controlled the dog thing, not the other way around. I would also like to know exactly what this "leash" was, how it was placed, how it was used. I had my suspicions, but was not sure.

Singh himself was a complete unknown. I had met him, but I had not seen the Singh who was now being described to me. They were talking of a guy completely at home with the supernatural and the world of the dead. I had never thought such things even possible.

By this time we were approaching the Chaguaramus beach area, just before the old narrow road to the abandoned hotel. We paused while Malcolm and the hound gave screaming horrors to a small group of night bathers. I began to see that my two companions, while not visible, could make their presence known, and the Fido thing was either slightly visible or maybe now-and-then visible.

As we resumed our journey, I asked about it. Roy looked just a little smug as he answered. "We sort of hit back of they talking."

I stared at him for a moment, not understanding. Then I realized that he meant they impinged on the subconscious, similar to my method of entering Jadine's dream world; but they did it to persons that were wide awake and not known to them.

They don't have to be physically visible, I thought. It's a matter of getting someone aware of them, and then letting their own imaginations fill in the blanks.

"Don' work on everybody," Malcolm said, "but some people sense we easy and scared people feel we too."

I thought about that. They give horrors or put a scare to the more superstitious, and the fear spreads to others. I filed away the information for future reference.

Then I stumbled a little, looked down and realized we had turned off on the old hotel road. This road was rough in texture, as if they had run out of the good asphalt before doing this road. Time is running out, I thought. I'd better pump these guys, as I might not get a chance later. I just wish I knew what might be important. Then I would know what questions to ask.

"Why is this Singh character safe from you?" I asked.

"He own Fido," answered Malcolm, "and he got our leash. So he very safe from we. He got no worries, man. About we he sure."

"He the top Obeah man in this area," added Roy. "He learned from he father, and he even went to Haiti to study more with the big boys and them in Obeah in Haiti. They real strong Obeah in Haiti and Mr. Singh good pupil. He very strong, Mr. Singh. He no lightweight, that sure."

I listened, still hopeful of getting something I could use. Clouds had filled the sky, and any scenery along the road was obscured by darkness. There were no street lights, no house lights, no road traffic, nothing to distract me. "He bring Fido back to Trinidad from Haiti," continued Roy, "and other things, too. Without Mr. Singh and Obeah, Fido have to go away or just stop being. Fido very loyal."

"Fido not dumb," added Malcolm.

"Can Singh see you?" I asked, "or does he depend on Fido to watch you? How does he talk to you?"

I listened carefully. Whatever I heard now could be important.

Sooner or later I had to deal with Singh, and we were rapidly approaching the sooner end of that equation. Know your enemy, I thought. Learn his methods. Determine his motives. Anything.

Malcolm seemed to be thinking about my last questions, and hadn't answered.

Roy answered instead. "Goes into ganga trance," he said. "Then he can chat with we direct. He use strong Obeah to protect he body while he in trance."

Ganga, I thought. That was what the Indians in Trinidad called marijuana. Live and learn!

That's a use for marijuana I never heard of," I told them. "I always thought pot just made you high."

"Special type," said Roy. "Not really ganga, but he smoke it in a pipe and he go in trance."

Still, pot, I thought.

We were now almost to the old abandoned hotel at the end of the narrow road. I could see the beginning of the long, wooden steps which led down to the beach area, about a hundred feet lower. There was a break in the cliff just before the parking lot, a break probably caused by a landslide or something like that. Whatever, it allowed me to see a small part of the beach area from our higher level. I could see a series of seven, smoking, yellow flares and two red. They were on the beach itself, and I knew their location had been dictated by their visibility from above. Realizing it was Singh, I found myself swiftly approaching a state of desperation.

Soon I would have no chance to escape at all. If I could break away, I might find a way to build strength, get to Jadine and find out what I'm really up against. She can help me determine what I can do and what I cannot do. She knows about these things.

"That he," said Malcolm, breaking my chain of thought.

I turned and ran like a rabbit away from the ocean. My brain just shut itself down for the duration, and I split. I wanted no part of what was to come next.

I made maybe a hundred feet, and then the dog thing had me. I turned to fight my way free and saw what Fido had become. I fell to my knees, whimpering, all fight gone.

CHAPTER NINE

Determination, planning, courage, these things were suddenly meaningless. This was so far out of my experience that my mind just closed in for the duration, and all I could do was wait.

Fido had grown, his body towering above me, his red eyes flashing fire, spinning, his yellow teeth gleaming with slime and filth, foam dripping from his jaws.

He clawed me a little, as if testing the texture of a piece of meat, then started tossing my unresisting form around in the air, like a kitten playing with its prey.

I learned first-hand what the claws felt like, as they entered my body and ripped through until they got a good grip and held firm for him to drag me in. Hot, searing pain shot through every nerve as his teeth gnawed and ripped. I did not have the ability to pass out from pain, that is something only the living have. I had to take it, with no way to avoid it.

What was worse, I felt his amusement and enjoyment as he ripped at me. Somehow his feelings of pleasure were transmitted directly into my brain where I could not escape them. I felt his delight, as each new torture was initiated.

Finally he shook me violently, and dropped me in a heap on the ground.

It was over.

It had happened quickly, and was quickly over, and, while something in my mind unhinged in pure unadulterated fear and panic, some other fragment of me was watching calmly and noting that there had never been the slightest intent to harm me permanently. This was an object lesson, nothing more.

I looked at the creature again, warily, although I knew I would not run again.

He had reverted to his accustomed size and sat watching me as if hoping I would try again.

He grinned, and it was clear it was a grin.

I was careful not to move.

My side felt as if I had bathed in acid, and when I ran my fingers along the area he had savaged, I felt long, deep furrows where his teeth had raked and gouged my flesh.

Malcolm and Roy walked up, taking their time. I noticed that Roy kept a wary eye on Fido.

"Shit," complained Malcolm. "He give up too quick. Fido not even get warmed up good. Thought we going to get a show. Too quick, no fun at all."

"You try run, and you stop quick, too!" snapped Roy. "You never tangle with Fido much. I have. That thing, he just mean is all."

"You ready to meet Mr. Singh," asked Malcolm, "or you want to argue with Fido some more?"

I got to my feet. "Not really much choice," I muttered.

"None at all," said Malcolm cheerfully.

We returned to the long, wooden steps down to the beach and started down. We could see the nine flares clearly, and soon I smelled the odor of marijuana—but with a difference, like a musty, rotted variety of pot, as if something dead had been mixed in with the weed.

Must be in the curing, I thought. But, still, pot.

I couldn't tell if the smell was from one of the flares or from one of the other smoky piles of herbs spotted here and there amongst them. Everything was arranged with care, everything had its place. These Obeah types carried their symbolism to extremes, but it seemed to work for them.

Sitting in the middle of the circle of smoke and wavering light and shadows was Singh, the same small and dried-up husk of a man I remembered. His face was shining with sweat, his naked body tense, his eyes rolled back in his head. Blood was smeared on his body. I looked around and saw a black rooster with no head carefully arranged near one of the flares. I knew the head had to be somewhere, probably part of Singh's careful arrangement, but I failed to find it.

I remembered Jadine telling me how chickens were involved in many of the Obeah ceremonies, and the head was always an important part of it. I shrugged. At least I knew where the blood came from on Singh's body.

As we approached, Singh's eyes became focused, and he watched us, plainly seeing all of us. He gazed at my torn shirt, at the shredded flesh visible through the tears in the shirt fabric.

"Ah," he said in that rasping, deep voice, completely inappropriate for so tiny a man. That was one of the things I had disliked about him from the start. "I see you chose to argue with my little pet," he continued. "I trust that won't happen again."

I did not answer immediately. I stared at him, at this man who had me killed. About this second life of his I had no inkling or, rather, had not believed it possible. I had been told, by Jadine, and I ignored her warnings, for this was not something easily accepted by Americans.

As I stood there, my temper flared.

He killed me, I thought. This little chicken shit had me murdered. I tried to jump for him, but my body refused to obey me. I remained rooted to the spot, and Singh did not appear to have noticed my efforts. I felt a burning near my left ear, in the back of my head, turned and saw the chicken head impaled on a thin bamboo rod, the open eyes on me, hypnotic. I turned back to Singh, still angry, but resigned. Whatever was next, there was no choice.

"I see you remember me," Singh said. "Not that it is any help to you. This is no longer your business world, Mr. Correy, and you are no longer real in that world. Now you are in my world, and it is not a world you ever imagined. Never mind that it was necessary to end your life to deal with you on my terms, that is unimportant. The important fact is that you are here, and you are mine."

Malcolm, Roy and the dog moved to one side and sat quietly, seemingly at ease with the scene.

I glared at Singh. "Pretty steep price you made me pay for a little bit of quarry rock," I said, "and dead or not, you sure as hell don't own me."

"Meaning you disapprove?" He chuckled. "Oh, my dear Mr. Correy, this is quite amusing. I suppose I should have anticipated your ignorance. The people of my country grow up knowing Obeah and what to expect from someone like me. You must learn. It's a little late for you, of course, but you will learn. This I promise."

"I don't see how you can force me to do anything for you," I said, my temper still in control of my tongue.

I glanced to the side. Roy and Malcolm talked with animation where they sat. The dog watched Singh and me intently.

"You can't even talk to me without killing a chicken," I growled, "and you seem to think you have some kind of control over what I do. You'd better think again, asshole.

You don't control shit."

"Oh, my," he grinned, "and you just argued with my little pet and lost? Don't you imagine I have other methods as well. I do not care what you think or what you might want. I never operate with volunteers. Too variable. I always use naked force and naked fear, and I never have to worry about loyalty. Absolutely never."

He had my full attention now. I fought my temper, for I needed to know what was going down.

"This world of mine is not like the world you left behind," Singh continued, "where good and justice prevail. In this spirit world, justice is what I decree at the moment."

It sounded to me like a pep talk, a briefing to the new boy on the block. "So how do you force your spirits?" I asked, hoping my presumed ignorance might bring some information."

"Many ways. For Malcolm here," he indicated Wormface, "I just allowed his face to become real for a few weeks. Since it was dead, like him, and since my little Fido was making him sit quietly at the time, the worms had a holiday. He was happy to promise anything to have his face changed back again. Of course, he knows how easily I can repeat my performance. Unfortunately, there was no way to undo the damage already done by the worms, but, at least, I could forestall further harm and allow the pain to come to an end for him."

Malcolm was watching us now, his eyes glittering, a half snarl on his face. He made no move of any kind.

"As for Roy," continued Singh, "he was much simpler. I just turn Fido loose on him occasionally. No problems."

Roy ignored Singh. His hate filled eyes were on the dog thing.

Singh grinned, a parody of a grin. "Of course, with Roy and Malcolm, neither of them have anyone still alive that means anything to them. Most of the others in my group react quite satisfactorily after I let my pets horrors their loved ones. Or after I threaten to do so. The threat is usually sufficient."

"What do you want done?" I asked. He had to have a program. He was too well organized to have all this set up just to take revenge on me. Malcolm and Roy watched us closely, listening, my last question evidently of interest to them.

"Oh, simple things," Singh said. "Protecting well-paying clients such as Mr. Maharaj from avenging spirits; haunting specified families by specific contract; helping my business interests by obtaining contracts, or higher prices, or by asking my competition to go elsewhere; eliminating political rivals for the politician who pays the most; any number of things. I have many interests."

I bet you do, I thought. I was staggered. I had thought about death many times over the years, but this whole thing was completely unexpected. For Singh, death and torture were tools for use in his business. Obeah was his business, and he was good at his business. Obeah was not a hobby, or even an obsession. It was something to be used to further his everyday business dealings. I watched Singh, waiting.

"As for you," he continued, "I have not quite decided. I might use you to persuade a few clients that they should deal only with me." He studied me for a few seconds, seemed to reach a decision of some kind. "Yes," he said. "I have a few uses. Meanwhile, I believe you might need a bit of softening."

He half turned to Malcolm.

"Malcolm, you and Roy will take our white man back to St. James, to his grave. I want him in his coffin, and we will leave my little pet to ensure he does not come out."

He returned his attention to me.

"Incidentally, the word Fido is very close to the real expression for this beast of mine. Otherwise, I might insist on accuracy. Now, I think three weeks of absolute solitude should suffice. Please return here in three weeks, and I will give further instructions. Now, be gone."

So far as Singh was concerned none of us existed any longer, although I had little doubt his displeasure would be felt if we did not "be gone" as he commanded. I remembered my dream from when I was still alive, when I followed Singh after being dismissed.

I did not object as Malcolm and Roy led me away.

Fido kept close.

I was very depressed by now. My prospects had deteriorated drastically, and my near future was not very bright; to be forced into my coffin with my rotting body, with Fido sitting on the ground above me daring me to move above the grave, raking me with teeth or claws if I took the dare.

It was obviously a common "softening up" procedure, and the dynamic duo had certainly set it up a few times before.

They had no difficulty letting me know how it would work, and they clearly felt it was effective.

On the surface it did not sound too bad, but I had read a great deal when alive, enough to comprehend that the particular punishment might be worse than the one dealt to Malcolm. Not worse in lasting effects, but worse in its effect on my ability to resist.

We reached the Chaguaramus beach area before any of us said anything, other than the general outline they had given me on what was about to happen. It was Malcolm who finally decided to talk about something other than their delivery of me to the Western Cemetery in St. James.

"What you think of Mr. Singh?" he asked.

I looked at him. Is he really curious, I wondered, or is he after information for his boss. I decided to treat it like a question from an acquaintance, to give it the innocent interpretation.

"I'm not sure," I said. "I expected the talk session to last longer. Doesn't seem to have been long enough for him to become acquainted with me, if that really was his purpose."

"That how he always do," answered Malcolm. "First meeting quick, quick. Second, long instructions, big get-acquainted, learn rules. In between, he place the leash, one way or another."

"You can' get away," added Roy. "No matter where you go, he know, and he send Fido or other things worse. If punishment not enough, there always friends of yours in world of living, like relatives, family, real people. He get at real people easy."

Yeah, I thought. He got at me easy enough.

By now we were past the beach area and starting to reach places with people again. My companions did not seem too interested this time. Did this business with Singh bother them, then, or were they in too deep for that.

"What sort of things does he have you do?" I asked.

"Generally making people do business the way he want and thing," said Malcolm. "Sometimes he want somebody humbugged to death as lesson to someone else. The bad ones are when he send Fido or other things with we. When he send they, we never know what he tell they. They get bored and sometimes they play with we. They play nasty. Mr. Singh, he no care if he pet play a little, keeps they happy. No never mind what we think."

This thing looked worse with each new revelation. I watched my two companions, but they did not display any strong feelings over what they were telling me. The dog thing just grinned.

I shivered. "There must be some way out."

"Wish there were," said Roy.

I thought hard for a minute. "What does he do for a leash if Fido's not scary enough and there's no relatives?" I asked.

Roy considered that, grinned a little. "He can get a piece of your dead body, even hair and thing, then he can do plenty. Getting piece of you real easy for someone like he. He generally have what he need before he ever talk to spirit. When he have these things he can use Obeah magic to make you weak so he pets or tame spirits can take you, or use magic to banish you inside a bottle or chain you to a rock under the ocean or—"

"All right," I growled. "I think I get the picture, but I still think there must be a way. He can't be omnipotent."

"Why not?" asked Roy. "He handling spirits, not people, and he not do anything that permanent to we, other than how we look and thing. Nothing ever happens to he and nobody ever notice he. He careful and all he do is borrow we. Nobody care thing like this with living, even less with we type. We dead now, man. You better 'member that. Everything change. Not like living world at all.

The rest of the trek was made mostly in silence, with erratic conversation. I learned that Malcolm and Roy and most of the rest of Singh's spirits stayed in St. James Western Cemetery between jobs for Singh, the same cemetery that held my body. Occasionally they were given free nights to prowl outside the confines of the cemetery, but such free time was forbidden without Singh's express approval. Singh sent Fido or some other such beast to fetch whichever spirit he wanted.

It was an existence unheard of by anyone still alive, other than persons like Singh, and it was an existence so bizarre that only the fact that I could see it for myself made it believable.

As we approached the cemetery, I tried, once again, to get these two to let me go.

Malcolm laughed. "That be stupid. Even if we turn you loose, Fido no allow it, and then we get trounced, too. So why bother?"

"Fido can't be very intelligent," I countered. "Beast, evil, magic, Obeah, whatever he is, he has an animal brain and can be tricked or outsmarted."

"Not too sure of that," said Roy. "He don' act like animal when he thinking. He demon, smart like hell. Better not think he like animal and thing 'cause then he outsmart you for sure."

"How about churches, religion. Does that slow things down?" I asked. I remembered my experience earlier, and wanted to know if this was a weak point that might be exploited. Maybe I could outrun these guys to the Church of the Nazarene. It was not that far.

"No," Malcolm replied. "You lucky first time on that church thing. Roy and me, we can't go in, but Mr. Singh he got plenty others can. And Fido, he can go in, too."

"Time to shut up," said Roy. "Here the Correy tombstone. Go ahead, Clark, man, get in your coffin and thing."

I stood for a moment, trying to stall, trying to think of an excuse, anything.

"What if I just refuse?" I asked.

Roy grinned. "Then Fido put most of your pieces in your coffin after he tear you apart. All the pieces still be like now, but hurting. Mr. Singh he put you back together later, sort of, but not good, like now. Sometimes Fido lose piece or two, and nothing fit right."

It was not the kind of argument that you pursued very far. Roy was too graphic in his description, and the Fido thing just stared at me, with a doggy grin and those pinwheel eyes apparently spinning just a little.

I moved into my coffin, and Fido sat above the lid on the surface.

My three weeks in hell began.

CHAPTER TEN

I determined later that it was late March of 1981 when I entered my coffin. I anticipated initially I could take away the torturous aspects by mind exercises, but soon it grew boring. I had not had the prior training such exercises required.

I moved up to the surface to see if Fido were there. He was, and I picked up a couple of new gashes in my back for my trouble. Later trips to the surface were more cautious. As boredom became more pronounced, I started exploring my limits, what this thing would let me do, and what he would not let me do. I determined the limits by pushing my luck until Fido reacted.

Teasing Fido invariably got me clawed or bitten, but it gave me some thoughts as to what this Obeah construct thing could do. Not a pleasant way of getting information, but I would need this data some day.

Besides, there was nothing else to do, nothing else at all.

I wondered what arrangements I might have to make to survive during this new phase of existence I now found myself in. I assumed that if I did what Singh wanted, within limits, I could get the prowling freedom my captors mentioned and conceivably work out a plan of escape with Jadine's help. I was not sure how, perhaps by having her move my body to the States. Even that, I knew, would be fought by Singh, and Jadine might be hurt. That I could not, would not, allow.

Still, the idea of moving the body out of Singh's reach held the most promise as a way out. I would have to be extremely careful, and it would have to be planned very cautiously. But it might be possible. There might be a way.

As the week progressed, I ran out of things to plan, things to worry about.

By the end of the week I was screaming and babbling, and I had several nasty rips in my chest and back from Fido's ministrations. He did not touch my face or arms, so I reasoned Singh must want those areas undamaged for reasons of his own.

The second week moved forward slowly.

Complete solitude is one of the most exquisite tortures there is. The only thing that preserved my sanity was my occasional foray against the dog thing. Those encounters always had the same ending, but they gave me reassurance that an outside world still existed. I was also beginning to understand that Fido's presence was a carefully planned arrangement. Singh could have forced compliance with absolutely no contact with anything, even a Fido type anything. However, he wanted his staff to be capable of thinking, of acting.

The second week passed.

The third week was the worst.

I was not screaming much by then and was very near insanity. My tirades and attacks against Fido grew less frequent, and, mostly, I lay still, watching what was left of my body, mostly bones and some patches of hair and dry skin here and there.

When Malcolm and Roy returned for me and had Fido move, it took me considerable time to comprehend I was free to leave the coffin. Then I boiled out of the ground in a rush, looking wildly about for an avenue of escape.

"Don' try it, captain," said Malcolm.

I saw he and Roy were waiting to one side, quietly, allowing me time to calm.

"Don' try it," he repeated. "Mr. Singh, he put you back in your hole if you run now."

Immediately I subsided, the threat enough to bring me completely in line. Right then, I would have committed murder to stay out of that coffin. Later, things would return to their proper perspective, but at that moment, fear of my grave was uppermost.

"Much better," Roy said, softly. "Mr. Singh, he ready to talk now."

I made several attempts before I could answer. My voice was almost ruined by the weeks of either screaming or the longer times when I did not make a sound. Why that should be the case for a spirit or ghost, I don't know. Maybe it was a memory thing, a recollection from my earlier life that could still affect me, now, through my mind.

Finally I croaked out my answer. "Same place?"

Malcolm grinned. "He talking, sort of. Took me almost an hour to get my voice back first time I go in hole."

"And you still work for him," I grated.

"No choice. Like to waste Mr. Singh, but he hold all the cards. Stupid to fight. No way to win."

"Time to go," said Roy. "Mr. Singh he wait."

"Why doesn't he come here?" I asked.

"Too many people see he Obeah flames," Malcolm replied. "He don' like complications. Wants everything smooth. He set up he shop where no complications at all."

"So let him wait a little," I muttered.

Fido was abruptly on his feet, growling low in his throat.

"Okay!" I said. "So we leave now. Mustn't make Singh wait."

"Smart not keep he waiting and thing," said Roy, just a little impatiently. "He have ways to show he vexed. No good, man. No good at all."

At the moment I could think of no answer. Singh said go, so we go. End of story. You can't argue with his type of persuasion.

So we were off, again, on that tedious hike from St. James through Cocorite and Carenage to the old army base at Chagauramus. Again, it was night. At least this time I knew what to expect, and I knew with a gut-wrenching certainty that Singh would let me know what he had in mind.

It was self-evident that Singh never permitted his recruits to make up their own minds, to decide their own fates. He recruited them, confronted them, and punished them. Finally, he would let them know what he would permit them to do for him. No questions, no variations.

We walked in silence at first, but my time in isolation would not let me stay hushed. I could not tolerate the silence.

"How soon before I get a night to prowl?" I asked. "Provided I do what he wants."

"You'll do what he want," Malcolm answered. "Time off to prowl between you and he. Got someone to horrors?"

He sounded interested. It was clear that the major explanation for the anticipation these spirits seemed to exhibit at the prospect of manufacturing trouble was that this was the only source of entertainment they were allowed. So they hassled the living every chance they got. It was all Singh would give them, so they accepted it.

"No," I said to Malcolm. "Not horrors. Someone to visit. I still have a wife, among the living."

He turned away, not bothering to hide his disappointment.

"After a few jobs with Mr. Singh, you get taste for tackling the real people," Roy offered. "Makes time pass. Sometimes fun."

I shuddered, remembering the bit of tackling they did on the beach in the Chagauramus area on our first walk. Nobody got hurt, but it hadn't been much fun to watch.

"Doesn't sound so great to me," I said, "scaring innocent people. If you have to do it for this Singh character, if you're forced, I can see some justification; but doing it for fun makes you as bad as him."

"It still fun," insisted Roy. "I like to see they run and scream. If Mr. Singh let me go, I do it plenty."

I tried to look indignant, or repulsed, but I could remember a certain enjoyment when I was working on Maharaj. Irritated at the memory, I forced myself back to the conversation at hand.

"Do all his spirits obey him as easily as you two?" I asked, curious.

"Not all," said Roy. "We good, man. We a damn good team, and we smart. He don' worry 'bout control and thing with we. If he have spirit he can't control he handle more special. He got three in bottles, two on chains in ocean off West Moorings. Used to be three in ocean, but one got called. Mr. Singh couldn't keep he. Other two been there for long time now."

Roy looked at me, as if gauging how much I would accept. Satisfied with whatever he thought he saw, he continued.

"He lets the ones in ocean get part real now and then, and the fish eat they faces. Real ugly, they. Better to do what he say, like we."

I walked without talking for a while, then asked, "What if Singh dies? Are we released then?"

"Probably," Roy replied. "Supposing he wife don' find out too quick. She Obeah, too. With Mr. Singh, he never dead yet, so can't be sure."

"It has to be that way," I said. "There's no way he could control if he dies, and he wouldn't be able to give control to anyone else."

"Truth," said Malcolm. "At least, part way, but little more compli- cated when Obeah in place. Sometimes death not an end for people like Singh and them. Plus, with spirits, what if he have you in a bottle or chained in the ocean when he dead? Then whatever Obeah find you can take you. If no one find you, you stay in bottle or ocean. Better hope you not in bottle when he dead."

Time passed. We talked, we walked. I caught a glimpse of a flickering light on the horizon, reminiscent of heat lightning. We were approaching the same general area where we last found Singh.

"Almost there," said Malcolm. "We see Obeah flambeaus soon. Then we see what you do for he. Maybe we get job, too. Maybe with you."

"Sounds great," I growled. "That's all I need, to have you two idiots glued to me."

Malcolm shrugged. "Least you know we."

I looked at him in surprise. It was a statement I was completely unprepared for, and he was right. Bad as these two were, I knew them. Any new companion Singh might choose to stick me with would be an unknown.

Finally I said, "Yeah. You're right on that. At least I know you."

With that, I no longer felt quite so alone. Terrible as they were, they were victims like me.

The flambeaus were completely visible now, through the land fault near the parking lot of the old abandoned hotel, the same seven yellows and two reds. I wondered if there were some reason for the colors and numbers, some protective spell, maybe, to defend Singh from us.

If so, it meant Singh felt insecure in some way, and if he were vulnerable I wanted to find out where that vulnerability lay.

Just knowing he felt unsafe was promising, but not enough by itself.

If things like Malcolm and Roy can't find a way out, what makes me think I can, I wondered, feeling a strong chill.

"Where does Singh live?" I asked Malcolm. I still felt myself shivering from that sudden chill. I recognized it as the chill of despondency, the harbinger of lost hopes.

"Don' know," Malcolm replied. "Obeah man don' let spirits know he real home or he name. They don' take chances."

"Then Singh is not his name?" I asked, wondering if this were usable information.

"No way," laughed Malcolm. "If you from Trinidad, you would know name important."

"So we're dangerous to them in some way?" I persisted.

This seemed an important point. To me, anything that hinted at Singh's vulnerability had to be important.

"For sure, we dangerous," said Malcolm, "but it don' do no never mind if we don' know they real name."

"I knew him when I was living," I said. "Not well, but I dealt with him."

"Not too well," grinned Roy. "You dead, he alive. Not only that, you still don' know he real name. You know the name he give you, and you met he only in office and thing. You know the same name we know. That name worthless so far as we concerned."

"Yeah," I muttered, my hopes frustrated again. I had thought these guys might know his name. I should have known better. "Nevertheless, there must be some way. There just has to be."

"Sure, but we never found it," Roy said. "Better get your head set. We be there quick now."

I looked up, surprised. I had been so intent on the conversation I hadn't realized we had reached the bottom of the steps, and we were approaching Singh. I saw his eyes roll back into place as he heard or sensed our approach.

He wasn't naked this time. He was wearing a white dhoti. Another rooster had given its all for Singh's ceremony. Again, the rooster had been black.

Consistent, I thought. What if he runs out of chickens?

Singh grinned broadly as we made the last few steps. He enjoys the hell out of this shit, I thought.

"Ah, Mr. Correy has returned, I see. I hope you've been comfortable these past few weeks."

"Quite comfortable, thank you." I was determined not to allow him to make me angry. "I trust you didn't have a long wait," I continued.

"I was not concerned," he replied. "Malcolm and Roy know better than to keep me lingering. They've been with me for several years now. They make a very good team."

"So I gathered, and so they've told me in nauseating detail. And, now you've given me my beauty rest, what happens now?"

He laughed softly. "Just a bit of work I have in mind. Nothing difficult, you understand. Of course you remember my rock quarry.

It was one of the reasons for your demise. I found your partner much easier to deal with, incidentally." He stopped, noting the flush in my face. "Ah," he smiled. "You didn't know I struck a deal with your Mr. Emby after your death?"

He chuckled, then laughed uproariously.

Roy looked our way, curious, then returned to his conversation with Malcolm. I watched Singh closely, incredulous over the topic of conversation. Sure, I was a little pissed over his making the deal, but what I found hard to understand was why he thought I would be interested in his business dealings. This asshole obviously considered the whole Obeah bit as a part of his regular business. I, as a potential tool in his Obeah practice, also became a part of his normal business. It's hard to think of magic and everyday business as connected, but this was definitely Singh's way of life.

Singh was talking again. "As I was about to explain, your former partner has a new contract with the government on a road extension in the Curepe area, and I would like to furnish the asphalt for his operations. However, he claims my prices are high and my material inferior. He made this statement in such a way as to cast aspersions on my basic honesty. Fortunately, no others were present to hear the accusations, so it was only between the two of us. Still, it is a most unfortunate situation, one which I would like to rectify."

"I see," I said. It sounded as if Charlie had fixed Singh up as good as I had, maybe better. Probably got stung on the gravel deal.

"Yes, indeed," Singh continued. "Like you, the gentleman is an American. For some reason, Americans seem to have a certain resistance to my trusted workers here. Lack of knowledge of our rituals and beliefs and underexposure to the folk tales and symbolisms of our Obeah rites, these seem to impart a certain degree of immunity for most Americans to spiritual persuasions. However, you also are an American, and you know Mr. Emby quite well, so my little problem will not be a problem much longer. A stranger he could resist, and his mind would tell him nothing was there. You are not a stranger."

I started to interrupt. His face reddened. Fido came to his feet.

"Please, Mr. Correy. I would strongly advise you not to interrupt me. My pet does not like it."

From the corner of my eye I saw Roy grinning at me.

"Now, please pay attention, Mr. Correy," Singh said. "In the spiritual world, belief is very important. With you, Mr. Emby would be more receptive, and, once the initial contact is made, by you in this instance, the early resistance or immunity should disappear. This has been true in the past and should so continue." His grin was back. "Yes, Mr. Correy. You are not the first foreigner I have recruited, although you are my first American. I felt this would be a good start for you since you know Mr. Emby. Besides, the job is simply to persuade."

"I'm to persuade Charlie?" I asked. "That's all?"

Singh nodded, still smiling.

"How am I supposed to accomplish this?" I asked.

"Oh, that should be no problem. You have already demonstrated your awareness of the proper methods in your handling of Mr. Maharaj. I arranged a little test to be positive, and you performed admirably, while demonstrating a strong imagination. All in all, I was quite impressed, enough to have my friends here make a call on you on your return from the United States."

I felt like I had been hit by a sledge hammer. Singh had been back of all the things happening with Jadine. It had not been Maharaj at all. Jadine's life had been put at risk just to make me go after Maharaj.

He laughed, watching the emotions on my face. I must have been very obvious in my surprise, and my sudden fury.

"Yes, Mr. Correy," he continued. "I arranged for you to visit Mr. Maharaj a second time after I learned of your earlier dealings with him. I also knew about your trip. Not too many manage such a journey. Tell me, did you stay long enough to accomplish anything?"

"None of your business," I growled. "Get on with your explanation of how I get through to Charlie."

"Very well," he answered, unperturbed.

Fido was perturbed, though. He didn't like his boss to be interrupted at all. I kept my mouth shut and stayed very still. Fido slowly relaxed.

Singh laughed, softly, watching both of us.

"As I mentioned previously," he said, "you already know many of the methods needed. This I know because Mr. Maharaj informed me how you visited his dream and tormented him before the more interesting fracas you had with my staff. He told me what you did to him during his dream and while he was awake. He was quite detailed in his descriptions. I listened, and was able to deduce what he must have done to get you after him. Not very smart of Mr. Maharaj, of course, but that's his business."

He paused, cleaned a bit of soot from one hand. He waited a moment more, then continued.

"So, you are able to enter the dream world, you have enough power to influence physical objects, and you can affect things like the tongue and ears of living persons. Believe me, Mr. Correy, these are feats usually accomplished by spirits only after long training."

He chuckled again. It sounded more like a clearing of the throat than any expression of amusement, but his eyes were crinkled with dry amusement.

"Yes, indeed," he said. "If I had to take the time to train you, Mr. Emby might well have gotten away with his insubordination. You see, then, why I have advanced your training schedule."

"What if I refuse?"

Singh laughed. "Really, Mr. Correy. You cannot refuse. After all, I am not asking you to kill Mr. Emby, only to persuade him." His face tightened, and his voice became harder. "But if I should say to kill him, I would expect your obedience there, also. This time I do not ask for death, but I do insist on your full cooperation and compliance with all my desires. Of course, if you should refuse, I shall send one of my pets to visit your beautiful widow."

He paused. "No real problem, is there?" he purred.

"No, no real problem," I grated, somehow holding my temper in check. "I'll tackle Charlie for you."

"Very good," Singh said. "I was certain you would cooperate. However, I must make it clear that failure is not tolerated. You have one week to ensure I have his signature on a contract. Otherwise, I shall have to provide for some punishment."

He was grinning again.

I seethed.

"I always punish for failure," he continued. "I set a time limit, and I will not acquiesce in non-success. Not performing within my specified time period is sufficient to classify your entire effort as wasted."

"Just leave Jadine alone," I said, my voice low and menacing. "Leave Jadine alone, or I'll find some way to get at you. You can't be immune from me."

"Mercy, such a temper. Admirable, really." He grinned broadly. "I'm afraid I am very much immune to you, Mr. Correy. Better check with Roy and Malcolm. As for the lovely Jadine, please set your mind at rest. My penalty concerns you, alone. I will approach your widow only if you refuse to help. I'm sure you appreciate the distinction and will make every effort in my behalf. One week, please. You will return here to me at this same time one week from now."

"I have this job to myself?" I asked, having seen the wisdom in bringing my feelings back under control.

"Yes, I believe so," he answered "Of course, Malcolm and Roy will drop around the Emby residence from time to time to be sure you are proceeding with your task, but they will not interfere. You won't even notice their presence unless, of course, you should need help or if they feel strongly you should have assistance, assistance which they could provide."

Roy and Malcolm had heard their names and moved closer where they could hear what was going on.

"I suppose you'll send Fido, too," I said. "Might as well make a real party out of this."

"No, I think not," he answered, a flush starting to appear on his face. "I have other uses for the beast you call Fido. Now, please, leave me."

"Roy and Malcolm are coming with me now? Just to be sure everything starts off as you want?" My voice dripped with sarcasm.

"No," he answered. "I have other duties for them at the moment. You know where your friend lives, you know what I require from him, and you know the time limit. Therefore, you are dismissed. Please leave."

"Better leave," said Malcolm.

Fido watched me, alert.

I looked at Singh again, and decided Malcolm was right. It was time for my exit.

I headed straight for Jadine.

CHAPTER ELEVEN

I had assumed I would have at least a few hours' grace before my watchdogs arrived to see if I were on the job. It was risky, but I wanted Jadine to know what had happened, to see if she had any ideas how I could get free of Singh, and to be assured she got whatever protection might be available to her on such short notice.

I also wished to obtain whatever information she could offer me from her personal store of superstitious knowledge, for a great deal of that knowledge was hard data I could make use of.

Roy and Malcolm had told me many things, but what I needed now was, more likely, to come from Jadine's folklore. I needed advice on how to use what these two spirits had already told me and on how to get free. I wanted to know what Jadine could do to guard herself. I would be happy for whatever she could give me on Obeah practice, on ceremonies, on beasts and spirits, anything she might know. I was not sure what information I required, so I would take anything and sort it out later.

I found Jadine in bed, and I was lucky. She was sound asleep.

Quickly, I moved into her dream and found myself in a brawl.

She was fighting with her father and two brothers, with me trying to help her. I possessed my dream likeness in time to take a terrific lash from a board wielded by her father.

As I got up from the ground the brothers disappeared, but her father was still beating her with the board. Quickly I disarmed him and banished him, then I tended to her wounds.

I didn't worry about any return of fantasy villains. They had been pure dream. I had made enough nightmare constructs for Maharaj to know the difference between dream and interference.

As the bruise marks disappeared, she looked at me, and I saw she knew it really was me, not the dream me.

"Clark," she whispered. "A little longer, and I wake up. Clark, boy, I worry when I don' see you in the States and thing, and then when I back for a while. You see the baby? You okay?"

"Yes, I saw the baby," I said. "No, I'm not okay."

"Singh," she said.

I nodded. "How did you know?"

"I didn't," she answered. "Not 'til now. When I said "Singh" as if I knew, the ties leave your tongue. So talk to me, Clark, boy, what happen?"

I outlined my problems with Singh and what I had to do with Charlie.

"Oh, no, Clark! Not Charles!" Her face twisted in anguish. "He been good to me. He been a friend."

"I can't help it, baby."

I showed her the ragged tears in my flesh from Fido and watched her cringe back in horror.

"You see, I have to convince him," I said. "It won't be too rough for him. It's only a small contract. However, it means pure hell for me if he doesn't do it. I can't fight Singh, not yet."

"No," she answered, more calmly. "No, you can' fight the Obeah man. They too powerful, Clark, boy. It better you for Charles than some corrupt spirit."

By now I was fully dressed, hiding my scars from her compassion. Her dream had its setting in our home, so we moved to my old den where we could be comfortable.

"All right," I said, as we got settled again. "I'll just have to tackle Charlie and hope he comes through for me. If he doesn't, I get punished, and Charlie has a dilemma he helped create. If he does agree, I get off scot-free, and, maybe, he does too. What I need to know is if there are any quick ways to get myself free of this mess. Any ideas?"

She hesitated. "Only way is move your body or kill Singh. Shaky on first, but kill he, and you loose for sure. With conditions, Clark, boy. It not a clean break."

"That's what I thought," I said. "Kill him or move my body. As for complications, I can worry about them later. I'm after basics."

I stared at the painting on the wall of the dream den. I had done it myself, back in happier times. It soothed me, a little. It was so ordinary and reminded me of the ordinary life I once had. I sighed.

"You know, right now I see no way to waste this guy," I said. "He's too well protected, and you can't just step in and arrange for moving my corpse yourself. Singh will be watching for anything like that, and he can come to you with his tame monstrosities all too easily. You don't have the built-in resistance guys like Charlie have. You're vulnerable and Singh will watch you like a hawk."

"What will you do, boy?" she asked. "You can' leave it like it is. He not asking much, yet, but that can change quick."

"Two things," I said. "One, I want you to try to find Singh's real name for me. These other spirits seem to think it's important, and he keeps it such a secret that I think somehow it might be a key, it might give me a way to beat him. I want his actual name, and maybe his address. Singh is not the real name, this I know for sure."

"Of course Singh not he real name," she said. "Almost all Trinidadians like that 'bout they name. Look me. I got three and only one for real. And listen, boy, why you want he name? You can' fight someone like he."

I watched her, disturbed. She had an idea as to how bad this Singh guy was, but she didn't realize how vulnerable we both were to him. And she didn't comprehend how strong a hold Singh already had on me. She had warned me many times about him, but this had gone far past the things she knew about.

"I can fight him if I know his proper name," I answered, "or I think I can. You say all Trinidadians conceal their name. I think this is a practical custom, to avoid problems with folks like Singh. However, if not knowing a name can be a form of protection, if all this secrecy is needed to keep most people safe, then who would need that shield more than someone like Singh?"

She had a stubborn look on her face. I sighed, seeing my time racing past.

"Just let me finish," I said. "We can argue it out later."

She shrugged, not happy, but resigned.

"Okay," I said. "Knowing where he lived might help, too, but certainly the name. If you can track it down for me, I'll have the information, at least. Then I can use it later if I see the opportunity."

She nodded, but let me continue.

"For the second thing, I plan to get Charlie to try to move my body to the States, hopefully without alerting Singh. That could get me out without having to fight."

"You be gone from me then," she said.

"You can always follow me, or get married again and forget me."
I was a little impatient, but this was important. She had to agree.

"No, Clark, boy. I never marry again." She grabbed me in a fierce
embrace. I responded, and frantically we made love, fast and violent.

It was time wasted, time I did not have. I should have been questioning Jadine, researching Obeah lore, learning whatever she could teach
me. I did not have the strength of will to turn Jadine down, and I don't
believe the possibility of saying *no* ever reached my conscious mind.

Dream or no, making love was the therapy we both needed, and we
took what we needed.

She purred in my arms after, snuggled close.

"I don' change my mind," she said. "If Charles get you out, I
follow. I go to States. I got visa, and the kids are citizens. I go States
and get green card."

I sat up suddenly. "You can't let Singh know you're going if you
do. You don't move the body, either. Leave that for me and Charlie.
Singh will have you watched. You keep telling me I can't fight Singh,
that he's too strong for me. Jadine, he's even more dangerous to you."

I grabbed her by the shoulders to emphasize my next words. "All I
want you to do is try to find Singh's true name for me and where he
lives. Do it with caution. Don't let him get wind of what you're doing.
Be careful."

"Clark, boy, you going to have Charles move the body, so why you
need the name?"

"Sorry," I said. "I thought you understood. I plan to have Charlie
move my body, so I can have an out, but if you get Singh's name,
maybe I won't have to leave." I hesitated, shrugged. "Remember,
Jadine, he's got a pretty good grip on me. If he can stop that move, or
everything else goes wrong, I need something to give me a fighting
chance."

"You got to be careful, Clark, boy." Her tears were flowing fully
now. Our conversation was deadly serious, and she was concerned for
my safety.

"Don't worry," I answered. "I'll be careful. I've had a taste of
Singh's punishments. However, ghosts are not well-equipped for

searching through public archives or for gathering information in general in the world of the living. You and Charlie have to do it for me. Talk to your uncle, Krishna, and maybe he can help too."

"I thinking," she murmured, " and I think moving the body safer for you. No big face to face."

"And maybe it won't work," I replied. "I've got to have more than that. I have to know that name. I've got to have another option, in case I need it."

I was getting very nervous now. I had been here too long.

"Listen Jadine, one more thing. When you talk to Krishna, tell him you need a guard. They're not foolproof, but they seem to be effective, and I want you to have that protection."

"But that going to keep you away, too," she protested.

"I know," I answered. "It still has to be done. Also do whatever is needed to seal the house. That one can be gotten around, but not easily. Then, every night at seven, you take off the guard and open the house for fifteen minutes. If I'm able to shake Singh and visit, I'll do it at that time."

The look on her face told me I was going to have to explain a little better. I sighed, started searching for the right words.

Abruptly, I was snapped from Jadine and felt myself flying, without any control over my movements, no control whatsoever. Then everything went black.

Slowly, I felt myself recovering, my strength returning. I opened my eyes, aware I no longer was moving and no longer was alone.

"Oh, man!" exclaimed Malcolm. "He wake up."

I groaned and looked around. I was on the back lawn of Charlie's rented house. Malcolm and Roy stood to one side, watching me, pleased looks on their faces. It was apparent that whatever had happened, to bring me from Jadine to here, was attributable to these two grinning clowns.

"Mr. Singh's spell to make he move work real good," said Roy. He turned to me. "Mr. Singh, he tell we you don' go straight here, like you told. He give we way to make you come here, quick."

I stood, a little shaky. "Wasn't any need. I would have been here in another few minutes."

"Maybe, maybe not," said Roy. "We don' care. Mr. Singh he say use spell if you not here, and tell you get to work. He don' say anything about hold off minute or two and thing. He just say you not here we should use he spell, and let he spell kick you in you ass and bring you here. He also say you in big trouble if we need spell. So, I guess you in big trouble, man."

"I was just a little late," I protested. "Lost my way." Inwardly, I fumed. I had screwed up, royally.

Malcolm laughed. "Tell that to Mr. Singh when you see him in one week," he said. "Listen man, word of advice and thing. You better start to take he punish serious. They bad. You never catch real thing before. What you got was standard "soften up" thing, that not punishment. You better take he punish talk real serious."

"I suppose you two are coming in the house with me," I snarled.

"No," he answered. "Mr. Singh say only if you need help. We just kind of wait around and watch. Make sure you don' leave again."

I shrugged and entered the house.

CHAPTER TWELVE

As I left Malcolm and Roy in Charlie's yard to do whatever they would to pass the time, my mind was in a turmoil. I had screwed up big-time.

I could not fault Malcolm and Roy. So far, they had been an escort and not much more. They had not done anything to me, or to anyone else that I had seen. I remembered my impression of evil, but, so far as I could tell, they were victims like me.

My instinct to visit Jadine had been good; I needed that talk session to firm up my own ideas and put her on her guard. But I overstayed. That was my screwup.

It was two o'clock on Friday morning. I had until the following Thursday night at eleven to convince Charlie he had to deal with Singh. Then I had to take whatever Singh decided to mete out for my tardiness.

Then, finally, I could find out what Singh's long-term plans for me might be. Also, if Singh rewarded for success like he punished for failure, and if Charlie let me succeed, then maybe I could hope for time to see Jadine and find out if she had any success learning Singh's real name.

I wandered through the cluttered house. Charlie was a widower. Like many single Americans in Trinidad, and some that were not single, he had a Trinidadian girlfriend who slept over in his bed once or twice a week. The house did not look as if this girlfriend did much housekeeping, and Charlie, obviously, did none.

I had met the girl a few times. She was Indian, and her name was Isha. She had appeared to be a pleasant girl, and not too interested in strangers. I had left her alone. Charlie had little to say about her, so I knew she came to his bed, but little more. It was not a big thing in either of their lives.

I noticed a light in his study and moved there. Charlie was still awake, working on some contracts. I stood behind him, watching, wondering if he would balk at what I had to ask of him. Singh evidently anticipated he would not give in easily, because he gave me a week, not one or two days.

Still, I had little choice. I had to follow through as ordered. The alternatives were too terrible.

Charlie finally rose from his desk, stretched, stacked his papers in some semblance of order, and moved to his bedroom. Isha was there, already asleep. Charlie woke her for some bed play.

I waited, rather impatiently, for them to go to sleep. I amused myself by moving things around the room, playing with the little powers that spirits have in the real world. Then I noticed Isha's eyes wide with fright. I stopped playing at once. I wanted them relaxed, not up all night.

They finally fell asleep, both of them, and I moved in on Charlie. It was an easy entry, and I had to suppose my recent practice with Maharaj and Jadine had made me more adept at this than I had realized.

Charlie was naked, and he was much better endowed than in real life. He was reliving the episode with his girl-friend, and doing a much better job of it in his dream.

Impatiently, I banished Isha from the dream.

Startled, Charlie looked around and saw me. Shirt and pants suddenly clothed him. "Clark!" he exclaimed. "Where the hell did you come from?"

"I'm dead, Charlie," I answered, "but I need to talk to you."

Sounds silly, I thought. What else could I do, though? It was a peculiar situation I was in, and I had no experience to guide me. Play it by ear. See how he reacts and go from there.

"Dream time," he muttered, disgusted. "I don't believe in ghosts, not even yours. Jadine told me you were in her dreams a lot, but I've tried to convince her it was wishful thinking, her mind trying to adjust to your loss."

I was starting to comprehend I had a problem.

"I am real," I said. "You just can't see me whenyou're awake."

He shrugged, moved to his chair in the corner of the room and sat down.

"All right," I said, irritated. "Play your silly games. I have something important to say, and you will listen."

"Sure, I'll listen," he said. "Then I'll wake up and forget all about it."

Same old Charlie, I thought. This might get tough.

"All right, Charlie," I continued. "I'll have to prove it to you when you wake up, and I will. Believe me, I will. And Charlie, you're not going to like the proof. It will be something you can't just dismiss out of hand, and I guarantee I will get past your unwillingness to believe. Meanwhile, I want you to keep your mouth shut and listen."

"Not much of an improvement over Isha," he muttered. "Uglier and not built right. As a dream, you're not much. I should be able to do better."

"Do you know Mr. Singh?" I asked. I was getting irritated all over again, and that little seed of worry had sprouted and was growing with great enthusiasm. "He owns a quarry," I persisted, "and I believe he wants to contract with you for asphalt to use on the road project you picked up."

"Shit!" growled the dream Charlie. "Now I dream about business. Damn!"

He woke up, lit a cigarette, picked up a novel and reached for the light.

Angered, I snapped the light on and off a few times, before he could reach it. Leaving the light on, I flipped his loaded ashtray onto the carpet, took the freshly lit cigarette from his lips, and put it out on his bedside stand. The odor of burnt varnish wafted from the table.

His eyes widened. "Clark?" he whispered. Then, "Shit, I don't believe this."

I broke his mirror. Not shatter break, just a single crack down the length.

"Okay, okay! I get the message," he said, in a soothing voice. "Take it easy. Let me go back to sleep, and I'll listen next time."

I thought that reasonable, and waited while he tried to calm himself for sleep. It was no use. He was awake for the night.

I shrugged, mentally, resigned to wait. I was not too discouraged, for he should be receptive next time. I grinned a little, proud of myself.

I could put on a fair show now, and without the long buildup I needed for Maharaj.

I returned my focus to Charlie, who seemed to be searching for me, for any visual indication.

"Good luck," I growled, knowing he couldn't hear me.

"Sorry, Clark," he whispered. "If that's really you, and I haven't gone off the deep end. Better luck tonight."

He went back to his study until time to leave for work. Frustrated, I moped around the house a while, then went outside to see if my watchdogs were still with me. They were, on the back lawn.

"Problems?" asked Malcolm, eagerly, sitting up. They both watched me intently.

"No," I answered. "Had to convince him I was real, but that woke him up for the rest of the night."

"That happen sometimes," said Roy. "Fun convincing they though."

I glanced at him. "For once, I have to agree. It was fun convincing him."

He grinned. "Told you humbugging fun."

Malcolm grinned too. "Let we help," he said. "You don' know how good we is at getting people to do what we want. Toss in a solid scare, maybe twist a tongue and thing. No shit, man, people give in quick when something looks like we toss in a scare and thing."

"Yeah, man," added Roy, with a half wistful look on his face. "Think on it, man. "Sure you no need we help? We damn good at it."

"It's my job," I snapped. "Singh told you to let me do it without interference."

Seeing the disappointment on their faces, and fearing I might be a little unreasonable, I added, "I know what I'm doing. I know this guy. Let me do it my way. Okay? If I need help, I'll yell."

"Okay, man," said Roy. "We let you. Mr. Singh he say give you chance to show your thing. If you need help, we know. No need for yell and thing. We always know like that, man."

I turned from them and went back inside. I wasn't feeling sociable.

It was a long wait.

Charlie did not come home until after seven that night. I rummaged through the papers on his desk but did not see anything interesting. Mostly it dealt with projects we had contemplated together before my death, and which he had followed through on since, plus a few jobs new to me. There was nothing I had not expected. Charlie was very predictable.

When he finally got home, Isha was not with him. He worked late in his study again, until almost one the next morning. He finally got up from his desk, mixed a stiff drink, and took the drink and a book to bed. He was asleep by two, and I entered his first dream.

This time he was fully clothed, talking to the dream Isha in his study.

I banished her, and took a seat in front of the desk. I still remembered how I had dealt with Charlie when I was alive, and I did not want to do anything out of character, afraid that might serve to convince him I was not real.

"So you're back," he said. "I hoped you wouldn't return at all. I have never believed in ghosts, and I'm not sure I care to change." He took a drink from a large glass near his hand. "At least, I'm willing to listen," he added.

"Very good, Charlie," I said. "I wanted to talk to you about the contract Singh wants you to sign, the asphalt for the road project, the one you just got the go-ahead on, the government project."

Charlie looked straight at me, the beginning of a grin on his face. "Right to the point, as always," he said. "I thought maybe you'd want to talk about what it's like to be a ghost or ask about Jadine, but you go right into business first. Being a ghost hasn't helped you learn your priorities at all."

The grin became larger as he warmed to his subject. "Shit! My partner dies and comes back and what does he do? Earth-shattering revelations, sober reflections on what might have been, long tears for his lost dreams? Not my partner, nope. My partner sits down and talks business. Damn."

"This is important, Charlie," I growled. "I've got to get through to you before you wake up again."

"Go ahead," was his answer, as he leaned back in his chair, getting comfortable. "It's my dream, but it appears to be your quarter. Talk to me. After your little sideshow of flipping ashtrays and busting mirrors I guess you've earned a listen from me. What about this Singh?"

"Why didn't you give him the contract?" I asked.

Charlie's chair dropped back to the floor with a solid thud. I winced, then relaxed and waited to see how pissed he was.

Charlie did not keep me waiting. "Because he's a thief, or, at least, he wants to be a thief."

"What do you mean?" I asked. Inwardly I groaned. It was starting to look like Singh had cut the ground from under me.

Charlie shrugged. "I went out for bids, like always. His figures were high, so much so that I called him to ask how he expected me to even consider them. He told me his product was very high quality and, therefore, worth a higher price. I asked for samples and had to agree. I was ready to sign, despite the high price, but my foreman convinced me I should check the asphalt plant itself, to see if there would be an adequate supply.

"And?"

"No good," Charlie answered. "I don't know where he got his samples, but it was not from his own asphalt plant. I told him to forget it, that his material was inferior and his samples rejected."

"Was the material that bad?" I asked.

Charlie barked a laugh. He was always good at that. I had never figured how he did it. "About average," he said, "about what I need, but not at his price. I could go higher for good stuff, but not for average."

He glared at me, as if I were to blame.

I just waited, listening.

Finally he continued. "What got me pissed was the cheap trick he tried to pull. I let him know I knew what he had tried to do. You know me, Clark. No way will I let some clown do that kind of scheme and think he's gotten away with it. I let him know in no uncertain terms."

I groaned again, not inwardly, my hopes dissipating fast. "Have you signed with anyone else," I asked.

He looked at me. He had been expecting this question. It helped make sense as to why I were here.

"Not yet," he said, "but I probably will next week."

"Charlie, I want you to sign with Singh." I was leaning forward in my chair, trying to show my sincere face, hoping.

"No way, Clark. Not with Singh." He stood, paced a little, turned back to face me once again. "After I turned him down, after I let him know I had seen through his trick, after all that, he showed up at the work site next day, still pissed to beat hell, threatening to use Obeah and all kinds of shit. He scared off my foreman and two laborers. I mean, this little dried up pissant of a man, he actually scared the living shit out of them. They're Trinidadians and seemed to know him, and they believed every word he uttered. They couldn't wait to get the hell away from my job."

Charlie's face had reddened, and he was almost yelling. Slowly he calmed, sat down once again.

"Now that pissed me off royally," he continued in a softer voice. "So I kicked him out bodily, and threatened to put the police on him. Clark, I want nothing to do with this guy."

I stared at Charlie a few seconds, dismayed by his vehemence, and by the depth of his conflict with Singh. Shit, Singh killed me for less.

That thought brought me back to specifics. Charlie was in more danger than I had thought, and I was going to have an uphill battle if I wanted to change his present mindset, if I could change it.

"Charlie," I said. "I don't have much time, and I'm in real trouble if you say no, almost as much as you. This guy can hurt me bad, even dead, and he can waste your ass."

Like he wasted mine, I thought. There was no other choice. I gave him the whole story, in detail.

"Yeah, I see the problem," he muttered, sitting quietly. "I've listened carefully, but it's not enough, not by itself. You're just going to have to give me a few days to think."

I decided to let it slide for now. No need to activate Charlie's stubborn streak. "All right," I said. "I guess I have no choice."

"What else?" he asked.

I grinned. I didn't even have to look for an opening. "Maybe one thing," I responded, "something that might get me away from this Obeah thing altogether. My thinking is that my only escape from Singh is if he dies or my body can be moved out of the country, out of his reach. I think this body-moving might have a chance of working." I gave him a brief description of my trip to the States and why I thought it was relevant.

Charlie did not look happy, for I was asking for a lot. However, I didn't see his stubborn look either, so I could hope.

"Well, I doubt you'd ask me to commit murder," he said, "so I assume you want me to move your body. It will be a pain in the ass with all the red tape, but it can be done.

Have Jadine give me a power of attorney, and I'll get it taken care of for you."

"It's not that easy," I said.

"Go on," he said in a resigned voice.

"Well, Jadine can't be involved at all," I said. "He's watching her, and there are too many ways he can get back at her. You can't be involved directly for the same reason."

Charlie brushed that last comment aside. "Except if I turn him down," he said. "Even if he does find out it's me and gets pissed, he can't stop me, and I can't imagine he'd try to hurt me physically over something like this."

"Charlie, I don't want you to turn him down," I said.

He was getting red in the face again. He stood up, started pacing, slowly calmed. When he finally resumed our conversation, he had his "let's be reasonable" look on his face.

"Clark, I didn't say I would turn him down," he said, "but I might. In fact, I would love to. Every instinct I have is telling me to tell Singh to go screw himself. But I also listened to you. You were a good friend, and your story was very convincing. So I haven't decided yet. Thanks to you, I now recognize I'm dealing with a dangerous situation, and that my decision is not just a simple business decision."

He paused. "As for the moving of the bones, I suppose you're right. I can't handle it directly, and I dare not go through Jadine. I still don't see any big problems, so stop worrying. I'll take care of it. Three weeks, maybe."

He finally sat down again. I sighed.

Three weeks! That has to mean he is going to give in on the asphalt.

"All right," I answered. "Listen, Charlie, I sure appreciate all of this. You'll let me know on the contract business soon?"

"A few days," he answered. "Now I have a question."

"Go ahead," was my reply. "I guess it's your turn."

"Have you been giving Isha shitty dreams also?" he asked. "She says she's been having dreams about me wading around in blue mud, and says that my skin is turning blue in the dream, then blistering and falling off."

"Not from me, Charlie," I answered, "and not from anything with me. My backups wouldn't be able to resist telling me if they had gotten into the act, and they would not have hit so light. No, Charlie, I don't know where her nightmare came from, but it wasn't from me."

He was leaning back in his chair again, relaxing. No more stress, time to gossip. "Isha says it means I'm being marked by Obeah," he said. "I haven't let her know how accurate she was, what with Singh and everything. These islanders are very close to this spiritual bullshit aren't they?"

I got up. I didn't feel up to the gossip routine. "Yeah, that's for damned sure," I answered. "Listen Charlie, I'm going to leave. I think we both want to think about what we're going to do, and then I'll get back to you. Or you can reach me almost any time. I'll be around."

"Sure, Clark." He watched me as I left his study. I guess I could have just disappeared or something but what the hell, Charlie's a friend.

I moved out of the fantasy world and then to Charlie's real study; to relax, to think about our conversation. It was not exactly as I had hoped, but not bad. I would have to convince Malcolm and Roy to leave Charlie alone for a while longer. It should not be a problem.

The bit about moving my corpse sounded especially encouraging, but it would be useless if Charlie decided to fight Singh and get himself killed. I knew Charlie was not persuaded, yet. Somehow I had to impress him with the gravity of his problem.

I wasn't certain what to think about Isha's dream, but it was probably like Charlie said. These people are so close to the spiritual world, she just sensed something.

I heard sounds from the bedroom and knew Charlie was getting up. Knowing, too, he would remember, but, almost certainly, discount his dream, I went back to the bedroom to reinforce his memory, to make sure he remembered the dream the right way.

I flicked his light switch, made his alarm go off again, and moved his ashtray from his table to his dresser, after first putting out the cigarette he had lit when he barely had his eyes open.

"Okay, Clark," he said. "I get the message." His face had turned chalky white, and he had to sit on the bed to catch himself. "I didn't really believe it, seems like a bunch of shit."

I threw his shirt at him, started to do more when I became aware he had turned whiter and his hands were trembling.

Mistake, I thought. He had been so cool in the dream world, that I had not been expecting this.

I worried a little, hoping his normal composure would take over before he had a stroke or something. I had forgotten he could afford to be cool in a dream. No one ever acts normally in a fantasy. The rules are different.

I watched as he slowly recovered from his shock. His color improved, and he began to get dressed.

I started to move from the room but noticed something different about Charlie, something unusual. I took a closer look.

I saw a faint bluish discoloration around his toes and near his ankles, and the skin was a little blistered, like an early case of athlete's foot. I remembered Charlie telling me something about a blue, skin rash. Isha had been dreaming about it or something.

I looked again, but he already had his socks on, so I guess he hadn't noticed the spots or blisters on his skin. I recalled Jadine telling me once how people receiving attention from Obeah types occasionally ended up with skin rashes and sores, always blue or black in color

Allergic reaction to a ghost, I thought, uncomfortably aware that maybe I was right.

I shook my head a little and moved into his dining room. I watched as he moved to the bathroom, to the study, to the kitchen, to the dining room, preparing to leave for work, even though it was Saturday.

By the time he left, he was still agitated but seemed okay, otherwise. I watched him drive off.

"Look like you give he a scare," said Malcolm.

"Yeah," I answered, absently. I hadn't noticed Malcolm, hadn't even realized I was outside. Roy walked over to join us.

"He going to do business and thing with Mr. Singh?" asked Roy.

I shrugged. "I don't know. He'll let me know in a few days."

"If he say *no*, we help," Malcolm said.

"Not yet," I answered. "You have to let me do it my way first." I went back in the house, leaving them standing outside

I didn't know if Singh told them not to enter unless I failed, but I was thankful they stayed outside. I wanted solitude to think, and they would divert my brain from any chance of useful thinking.

CHAPTER THIRTEEN

I visited with Charlie several times the next night and again on Monday night. The blue rash grew worse. He started to scratch it while he slept, and by Monday night it was in evidence on the dream Charlie, too. He said nothing about it, as if he had not even noticed it, so I kept my mouth shut.

We avoided talking about Singh. Instead, we discussed Jadine and the children, my children in the States, and his business dealings and holdings. It was almost like our conversations before I died, long, rambling discourses on family, world events, Trinidad peculiarities and how they affected business, and other such things.

On Tuesday evening, he brought home a letter from Jadine to Elizabeth, my daughter, that he had written, and a power of attorney form, both of which he wanted Jadine to sign and then mail. He sealed both in an envelope, after making sure I saw them by asking me to flick the lights. He placed the sealed envelope in a desk drawer, closed the drawer, and made no further reference to the subject.

Isha had come back on Tuesday night and spent the night with him. Despite my impatience, I let him have his privacy that night. He had asked me for that on Sunday, and I had agreed.

I still came in the bedroom, telling myself I had given him his privacy by not entering his dreams. I wanted to listen, to hear what Isha might have to say about the blue rash, which had now spread to his stomach and back.

She said nothing.

I saw her studying the rash, with a serious look on her face. Charlie did not seem to be aware of it at all. He scratched it, rather absently, but, somehow, did not appear to notice it.

Weird, I thought. How bad does it have to get before he notices? Why doesn't someone tell him about it?

On Wednesday night, I visited his dreams again. He was waiting for me in his study, sitting comfortably, a drink in his hand.

"Well, Charlie?" I asked. "Have you decided?"

"Yes." He set his drink down, obviously ready for serious business.

It would not be gossip this time.

Good enough, I thought. It's high time.

I decided to get right to it. "Before we start, Charlie, I should caution you. Two ghouls I called Wormface and Bashed Head when I first met them, for obvious reasons, have been waiting outside. Their real names are Malcolm and Roy, but the descriptive nicknames are more apt, and probably fit their personalities better. They're here to watch me, but if you say *no*, they'll be after you strong. And I do mean strong. They are not pleasant to look at, and they love haunting."

"Sort of a backup team?" he asked. He did not sound surprised or alarmed. "You mentioned them before."

"Charlie, look." I projected an image of Malcolm and Roy, with all their faults highly visible and even exaggerated a little.

"That's the backup?" Charlie asked.

"Yeah, in living color," I answered. "Sorry about using the word *living*. It has been a long time since that word applied to them."

"Cute little buggers," he commented.

Come on, I thought. This is serious business. I shut off the images.

Charlie waited for my attention. I nodded.

"I have your papers ready for Jadine to sign and mail," he said. "You saw them?"

"You're changing the subject," I said. I knew now what he had decided, and I didn't want to hear it.

"I know," he said. "I'll get to your answer next. First things first. In those papers, I asked Elizabeth to deal directly with a friend of mine, not me. I'm not telling you who the friend is, your protection." He looked at me, a funny look in his eyes. "Also his protection," he added.

"Now," he continued, effectively shutting off my automatic protest. "Once these papers are mailed by Jadine, neither she nor I will be involved again. You'll have three weeks, more or less."

He scratched, absently.

"Okay," I answered. "Now, what's your decision?"

"Wait," he said. "I'm not through yet. Listen carefully. Somehow you'll have to evade your friends and warn Jadine. I mailed the papers this morning. All she has to do is sign the letter and the forms when she gets them and mail everything to Elizabeth. That's it."

I nodded. "Okay, so you've decided to fight Singh and you're making sure this business of mine won't get loused up if you're hurt or something."

He grinned tightly. "My life, my decision."

"Well, what do you want me to do?" I asked. "Go tell Singh now? My friends outside probably will want to try their luck with you before letting me do that."

He grinned again. It was not too pleasant as grins go, and I could see a lot of anger in it. I could also see that he was getting a charge of satisfaction out of this, maybe even enjoyment.

"Look, Clark, now it's between me and your Mr. Singh. You're out of it. As for your lovely, little playmates outside, just do one thing for me."

"Anything," I said, with feeling.

"Tell them I've agreed to meet with Singh at my office tomorrow at eleven in the morning. I already have him on my schedule, and he's been informed and has agreed to the meeting. I plan to turn his ass down again, then, and you're off the hook."

"I wish you'd change your mind," I said.

"You know me better than that, Clark."

"Yeah, I guess I do," I answered, a little sadly.

We talked a while longer about unimportant things. Then I left him and sat in his living room, in solitude.

It was four o'clock in the morning.

Thursday.

I went outside to find Malcolm and Roy.

*   *   *

It was an unpleasant conversation that followed, but I convinced Malcolm and Roy that Singh had to be informed of Charlie's decision, that he had to know before Charlie gave him his answer personally at eleven. I wanted them to think Singh would not want them to do anything until he had heard Charlie out. Most important, I wanted them to leave me behind.

I wished to let Jadine know about the mail she was to get, and I needed to be there before she woke up for the day.

"We all go," said Malcolm for the third time.

"No," Roy told him, surprising me, because it was an abrupt change of mind.

"Clark right," he continued. "We go, he stay. We tell Mr. Singh. We use Fido. He good messenger. We catch Fido at cemetery, and he tell Mr. Singh. Then Mr. Singh he tell we what to do, through Fido. Don' need Clark. He just slow we down." He turned to me. "You stay here, inside. If your friend pull double-cross, we come back and we horrors he until he do right."

"What if he try to run?" asked Malcolm, pointing at me.

"Who? Clark? You making joke, man." Roy laughed, continued. "Where he going to run? Where to? He got no place to hide."

Malcolm glared at me, not happy with Roy's decision, but not certain how to argue the point.

"Then we better go," he said, finally.

He looked at me. "Be sure you stay," he told me. "You already got one punish coming, man. Number two be bad."

"I know," I muttered, hiding my impatience.

They left.

I went back inside, making sure they saw me. When they had time to be truly gone, I came back outside.

It was almost four; I did not have much time. If Jadine got up early, I would have to wait for tonight, and if this Charlie business went sour I most likely couldn't come tonight. It had to be now.

I ran down the dark streets, pushing myself, and reached my house at five.

I found her still sleeping. I quickly unplugged her alarm clock, and entered her dream.

She was fighting a huge cat, her father to one side with a stick to hit her every time she managed to free herself. There were signs of four or five bites on both arms, and many scratches. The cat was rabid.

I banished her father and the cat, then took away the injuries. I was in full control before I had time to think about it. No finesse. No soft handling.

I took on her dream landscape and dream characters and bent them to my will with no delay. We moved in the house, lay back on the bed.

Might as well be comfortable, I thought.

"Clark," she whispered. "Why I always have such miserable dreams about my father? He dead, Clark. He was nasty alive, and he more nasty dead."

"Your dream wasn't caused by your dad," I said. "It was just a nightmare. I guess you had it too rough growing up. It's how your mind copes with the memory." I shrugged. "It's how it works. Now, listen to me. I don't have much time."

She sat up, waiting, sensing my urgency. "What is it? Is something wrong?"

"Hush," I said. "Just listen. Charlie is mailing you a letter and a power of attorney for Elizabeth. You have to sign both of them and send them to her. Get them in the mail as soon as you get them. I won't get another chance to warn you."

"To move your body?" she asked.

"Yes," I agreed.

"I thought you want Singh's name."

"I do," I said, but this is probably our only chance to start this. You can always stop it later if you get the name and it does anything for us. This will give me something for just-in-case."

"Why the big rush, boy?" she asked.

"Hush, girl," I answered. "Just do it. That idiot Charlie is going to turn Singh down.

"Singh, he can' blame you," she protested.

She tried to get up, but I stopped her. It was harder to get excited lying down.

As she settled down again I told her she should know better.

"You know these Obeah type people," I said. "Fairness is not part of their makeup, and Singh is typical in that respect. So just try to get Singh's real name for me, and mail this stuff off. This whole business is out of control."

She nodded, staying calm, but the fear was plain in her eyes.

"Charles was supposed to help me on name," she said. "Maybe I get Krishna to take over and thing. Charles may be too busy to bother."

"That might work," I said. "Listen, Charlie is awake, so maybe you can call him and explain to him how dangerous this is. Perhaps he'll listen to you."

"All right, I try," she said, in a very small voice.

"Good," I answered. "Now I have to go. I want you to wake up now and make that call."

She woke, sat straight up in bed, staring wildly. She stood and moved to the telephone. She waited a long time for an answer.

"Hello, Charles? Yes, boy, this Jadine. Clark told me to call you." She listened. I could hear the tinny echo of his voice.

"Yes," she said finally. "He was here. Still here. He say Singh going to hurt you bad if you turn he down and thing. Clark he tell me every-thing. Please Charles, don't fight Singh."

Another long wait as she listened. "All right. I tell he. Goodbye, Charles."

She hung up. She couldn't see me, but she looked straight at me.

"No luck," she whispered.

I could not wait. It was after six. If Malcolm and Roy had already contacted Singh, then he might have sent one of them back to keep an eye on me.

I left.

CHAPTER FOURTEEN

It was almost seven when I hurriedly let myself into Charlie's house. There was no sign of either Malcolm or Roy. Charlie was not home, probably gone to pick up Isha. I went to Charlie's study to wait. Charlie returned with Isha, stayed an hour or so, and left again.

Charlie just could not get the idea into his thick skull that Obeah was real, ghosts were genuine, and he was in deadly danger. He was reacting with good, solid American instincts, but this was Trinidad, and those instincts might get him killed.

As time passed I got more and more nervous, confusion clouded my thinking. I couldn't concentrate, I couldn't relax. I was going straight up the wall.

The time crawled; eleven, twelve, one in the afternoon. The house remained quiet. Isha moved upstairs, probably for a nap.

At half past four, the door banged open! It was Charlie. His shirt was half off, his hair a mess, his eyes wide with fright. Blood dripped from a nasty cut on one cheek. A huge, blue spot covered the other cheek and oozed a mixture of red and bluish liquid. It looked as if the cheek had touched a very dirty meat grinder.

Suddenly he flew the rest of the way into the room as if pushed. He stumbled, and fell across the couch. I rose from the chair as Malcolm and Roy boiled into the room behind Charlie and slammed the door shut. Their faces were wild with anticipation.

"For God's sake, I'll sign!" Charlie screamed.

I moved across the room, not really anxious yet, thinking they were just excited.

By the time I was halfway there, Malcolm had kicked Charlie in the face, and I saw his nose flatten slightly, then start bleeding. It was apparent it was broken. He scuttled across the floor toward the kitchen, crab-like.

I stood there, shocked.

Malcolm laughed, snapping me back to the present, to the suddenly escalated confrontation.

"Hey!" I yelled. "He said he'd sign. So cut out the shit."

"Look," said Roy. "He waited. Told you he would. Told you he no bug out on we. He good little ghost. Mr. Singh he wrong; first time I ever see he wrong, but he wrong this time. We find he right where he suppose to be."

"Come," Malcolm said to me. "Mr. Singh, he say you have to help we with this guy."

"No way," I said. "It's not necessary, not any more. He said he would sign. You heard him. Charlie said he'd sign. Leave him alone. We got what we're after."

"Too late." Roy grinned. "He tell Mr. Singh no and curse he real bad. Mr. Singh, he vexed. He fed up. He tell we he don' want contract no more. He tell we to fix he up good. He say you have to help we. He say if you not here use spell again. He say you probably fight we and for we to fix you, too, if you do."

He grinned again. "You going to fight we or help we?" he asked.

"You're going to kill him if you keep on this way," I said.

"Right," said Malcolm. "We going to kill he. Mr. Singh fed up with he. He say for we to fix he permanent. He want he dead."

I moved toward them as Roy hit Charlie with a heavy glass ashtray, hard enough to knock him sprawling again and bring blood oozing from the side of his head. Charlie had reached the kitchen while we were arguing, but, if he thought it was all over, that ashtray had changed his mind.

He howled.

I could hear Isha screaming from the top of the stairs, so she had heard the commotion and hurried to investigate. She would know what was going on.

Malcolm giggled, and Roy moved to intercept her.

"I'm not going to let you murder him!" I said. "He's my friend, and Isha never did anything to Singh."

"Better not try to stop we," Malcolm said. "Mr. Singh, he get very vex. Very bad for you he get vex. You already got troubles with he. Better you leave we to do we thing. You get he vex at you, and you never want to see he vex again. Stop now, and leave we to work. You got trouble if you don' help, but big trouble if you make it hard for we."

"Screw Singh!" I screamed, and grabbed for Malcolm.

We grappled, then I found myself thrown across the room.

I heard Isha scream again and looked up in time to see Roy beating her in the face with an metal bar of some kind. She fell down the steps, her face bloody, and lay still. Her eyes were open and staring, glassy with death. Malcolm was ripping off Charlie's clothes, piece by piece, giggling. Roy came down the stairs to help.

Charlie was screaming now, trying to pull free from Malcolm.

"My God, Clark. If it's you, please stop. I'll sign anything. Oh God, I didn't know you meant this kind of shit. Please, anything."

I staggered to my feet, closed my fist over the heavy rock Charlie used as a doorstop, and dived at Malcolm, smashing his head with the rock. He fell to one side. I jumped at him again but was kicked to one side by Roy, who hit me in the head with the metal bar as I fell.

"Very stupid," he said. "Mr. Singh, he no like this. You make job hard. Better stop, better not fight we any more. You suppose to be part of this team, fearless leader and thing."

As I tried to get up, Roy hit Charlie in the arm with the metal bar, which I now recognized as a piece of reinforcing steel. The bar got Charlie just above the elbow. I heard the bone snap.

Charlie staggered, tried to run for the door, and was felled by Malcolm with the heavy ashtray. Then they had the rest of his clothes off, and Roy maneuvered to jam the rod up his rectum.

I shook my head, getting my thoughts clear again. These guys were deadly, and they were fast. They did not tire. No matter what I did to them, they recovered. Of course, I did, too, but this was not something I noticed at the time.

I saw their speed and determination, and knew I had to act with just as much speed and determination if Charlie were to have even the slightest chance.

I flew across the room and hit Roy with one knee, sending the reinforcing rod clattering to the floor. I scuttled across, grabbed it, and managed to knock Malcolm flying again.

"Fool!" Roy circled me warily. "Mr. Singh he going to chain you under the ocean. At least. Maybe he do other things, too."

"He's got to catch me first," I answered.

I moved to keep facing him as he continued circling. Malcolm was

up again, attempting to get behind me. I feinted at Roy with the reinforcing rod, then knocked Malcolm down again.

Charlie, half recovered, made a wild scramble for the door. Roy left
me, grabbed Charlie by the balls, and flung him across the couch. I
came at Roy with the steel rod and he backed off.

Malcolm was up once more, but this time he headed for the door.
Roy looked at him, questioningly.

"I get help," Malcolm said, and he was gone.

Roy grinned at me.

"You in trouble, man. Now you beyond doubt in big trouble. Mr.
Singh he no like way you handling at all. We doing we job. You interfere. He be real vex. You dead meat, man. You in trouble like you
won' believe. Hoo boy, Mr. Singh he going to be super vex."

I continued to circle, hoping for another opening. Roy kept press-
ing, stopping occasionally to kick at Charlie, who crashed about the
room as if he were blind.

Then everything became quiet as Charlie discovered the body of
Isha at the foot of the stairs.

Roy giggled.

"No more pussy. Dark meat gone bye-bye. He have to take turns
with the worms now."

Before I could stop him, Roy was on Charlie again. When I
knocked him free, he had Charlie's right eyeball in his fist. Charlie
was screaming now, clutching in panic at his face. He no longer had
to act blind. With all the blood on his face and one eye gone, he was
blind. This time for real.

Now Roy was off-guard, so I caught him full in the side of his head
with the steel rod. All too soon he was up again, apparently undamaged.

It was increasingly clear that none of my injuries or his were endur-
ing. We could stop each other for a short time, but not permanently.
We could, in fact, pound each other all day and all night, and neither
of us would be any worse off.

"Malcolm back soon," said Roy. "He bring help. Maybe Fido. Then
we finish Emby and take you to Mr. Singh. He fix you good."

He lunged at me, missed.

"We can fight all day, you know," he said. "No never mind. Never tire, never stop. Mr. Singh he say fix Emby and you stop we so far. We no kill he, and you no stop we. Something have to change, quick. Mr. Singh, he going to be pissed real bad. He be plenty vex this time. He be fed up."

I had been listening, my guard dropped slightly. Charlie immediately paid for it by getting kicked in the throat.

The front door banged open, hard enough to splinter the wood, rough enough to tear a jagged chunk out of the wall. Malcolm and Fido entered the house. Fido grew until he seemed to fill the room, and even with only one eye, Charlie saw him.

Nothing else could have caused the look of pure horror on Charlie's face. The front of his pants grew dark as his bladder let loose. Fido reached down and the screams were unforgettable as the demon thing savaged him, shaking him like a rag doll.

I slumped to the floor, waiting for the carnage to finish, waiting for my turn.

It seemed to take a very long time.

The screams went on and on. I had never heard anything like this, not ever.

Then the screams stopped, and I heard Charlie's body thump to the floor. It became very quiet.

I knew he was dead.

I stayed where I was, too terrified and too discouraged to move.

I waited.

I saw no sign of Charlie's spirit.

I continued to wait.

"Smart," said Malcolm. "He not fighting. He nice and quiet."

"Maybe we let Fido have he anyhow," said Roy, hopefully. "Good fun. Fido play rough."

"No," said Malcolm. "Mr. Singh he don' like that. He tell we bring Clark fellow back with no damage to he. Wants he at the meeting place tonight. He say we keep he with we 'til then. He say make damn sure he no get away."

Roy looked at me. "Fight some more?"

I shook my head. "No, I won't fight. No reason for it now. You already killed my friend.

Roy shrugged. If he had grinned or smirked, I might have tried my luck again. I continued to sit on the floor, too dispirited to move.

I watched Fido leave; it didn't seem important any longer.

CHAPTER FIFTEEN

Roy and Malcolm sat near me, facing me.

"Too bad," said Roy. "Your friend, he shouldn' vex Mr. Singh like that. Very dangerous. Long time we don' see Mr. Singh vex so bad. Your friend, he not very smart. You not smart, too, but you strong. Long time since we need to get help and thing. But you still not smart. Mr. Singh, he too much for we, and too much for you. You fighting fire with pitch oil, man."

"We learn better and thing," added Malcolm, "but we in trouble, too. Mr. Singh he no like when we need help. He don' like that at all."

I looked up, wondering why they were acting so friendly. I had just been trying to batter them senseless, and they acted like that made no difference.

"Tough," I growled. "Maybe he'll put you in a bottle, too."

"No," came the answer, from Roy this time. "We too good a team. He just give we a little punish. You, now, he give you a real fix."

"So what do we do now?" I asked.

"Wait." Malcolm stretched a little, getting more comfortable. "Too early to leave for meeting with Mr. Singh. He don' like to wait, but he don' like we get meeting early, too. He want we on time. Not late, not early. He funny like that."

"Wait here?" I asked.

"Sure," said Malcolm. "Good as any other place. Quiet now."

It felt a little obscene. My best friend is murdered, and I quietly wait around with his killers because it's quiet.

Malcolm was studying me, as if he wanted to say something, but was unsure.

He appeared to make up his mind. "We ain' vex, man," he said. "You fight you own team, but you new, so we not vex. Working with Mr. Singh, we spirits at least no fight each other. But you don' know better, so we not vex."

I looked at him, incredulous.

They actually believed I would forget all that has happened and forge ties of friendship with them, and others like them.

I did not trust myself to say a word.

"Real quiet," said Roy, apparently satisfied with my reaction to Malcolm's words.

I had enough sense to leave that where it was, let them draw their own conclusions. But I had to say something, make some kind of comment.

"It won't stay quiet," I growled. "With all the screaming and commotion, I would imagine someone called the police."

"Likely," said Roy. "Maybe we humbug they, too. Mr. Singh he no say no on that. So maybe he want message out and thing."

"Good fun, bobbie-lund," Malcolm said. "Last time I humbug police, he shoot he friend trying to get me. Mr. Singh he had me almost visible, and police he shoot what he think he see. Bullet go through me and into he friend. Bobbie-lund, he still in jail. Manslaughter. Carelessness. Don' know charges for sure, but he still in jail and thing. That for sure."

"What did Singh have against the policeman?" I asked. My curiosity had overcome some of my horror and grief. I mean, Charlie was good people, but I had warned him over and over. He had known what he was getting into. He had chosen not to believe, but he had been told.

Also, I still had to survive, which meant I'd better try to keep some kind of communication going with these two, regardless of how I really felt about it. It might be very important to me before this whole mess was over.

"What did the policeman do to Singh?" I repeated, a little louder.

It was evident I hadn't been heard. I guess Malcolm was reliving his memories of his escapades with the police since he died.

"Gave he a bad drive ticket," came the answer, finally. "Made Mr. Singh lose license for six months. Most bobbie-lund know better, most learn who Obeah pretty quick. This guy new, didn' know Obeah going on. So we fix he."

"For a traffic ticket, one man dies, and another man ends up in jail for manslaughter?" I was incredulous.

Malcolm saw nothing unusual here. "Yeah," he continued. "Like I say, Mr. Singh get vex, he no make joke. Not he, man."

Malcolm looked me straight in the eye. "Mr. Singh he can' kill you, but he don' waste you if he could. He use you. He just give you punish and make you do things you don' like, like police thing. Pretty soon you do what he say all the time, fast, man. Then you learn to like, too."

I noticed a movement in the room, near Isha's body, like a sudden draft.

"That Emby," Roy said. "No see he yet, and he no see we. Too soon for that. Maybe later, maybe never."

"I thought violent death always gave potency to a spirit," I said.

"Not always," answered Roy. "Mr. Singh he say belief a part of it, too, and a mind strong enough for the change."

"Is Isha here too?" I asked.

"Naw," said Malcolm. "She long gone. She from Trinidad. She die, sense we in room, and she split. Don' want to get involved with we even when she dead."

"Can't blame her," I growled, my anger over what had happened rekindling.

Malcolm looked a little irritated. "You can get vex at we all you want, but he tell we do thing and we do and no one care what you think. Mr. Singh he get he way, and he happy. We want he happy."

I didn't care to hear excuses, if that's what this was, but I was interested in Charlie's spirit. Maybe we could do something between the two of us.

"Will Charlie get better at this?" I asked. "He seems to be having trouble getting into it."

Malcolm laughed. "How long it take you to be able to do something? How long before you could see we, before you could do the dream thing?"

I looked at him, thinking. "Weeks," I answered. "Yeah, it was at least a month, four or five weeks."

No immediate help, then, I thought. What I need is someone who's been dead for a while.

"You know, Charlie had a girl friend that died a year or so ago," I said. "An American. She was buried in the Western Cemetery in St. James, just like me. Marion Fields, I think her name was."

"Hey, man, we know Marion," said Roy. "She fun to work with."

"Yeah?" I said.

So much for Singh's statement that I'm his first American. The guy lies like crazy. He also told me Charlie and he had only a mild argument. I'll have to watch everything he says. Immaterial, I thought. Marion, that's my target now. Have to disguise it a little, don't want them to know she's my main interest.

"Well," I continued. "Charlie was real close with her, and, if he ever gets stronger, maybe she could get the message to him that I want to see him. I can't seem to get around much, but you guys could talk to her, have her give Charlie that message for me." I hesitated. "I wouldn't mind talking to her, either."

"Sure," said Malcolm. "We tell she. We tell she, and she talk to Emby and thing. She always know where Mr. Singh have we, so, when he can talk and thing, she can send he to you. Up to she if she want to talk to you sheself."

"Thanks," I said.

"Sure, man," he answered.

I looked away, tried to stay calm, dropping the subject quick before they could see how interested I was. I thought about what I had heard, how Singh handled things, how the spirits had contact between jobs. I wondered how I could use this information.

I'll have to learn how to obey a rule or two with Singh for starts, I thought. I must be more circumspect, for Jadine's sake, at least, and to get more freedom of movement. I frowned. I must control myself in future. If Singh permits me to have a future.

However, I didn't have any control on what Singh does, so I might as well not worry about it. If I could work something out, so be it.

My idea that Charlie might be able to help me seemed pretty unlikely now that he was dead, but I had done what I could for contact later. He might, yet, get control on himself, and he wasn't tied to someone like Singh. If not, maybe I could meet with Marion. I hadn't known her well, but maybe it would be enough.

For now I was on my own, and, except for Jadine's help, it seemed likely to remain that way. I would have to keep my temper in check to be able to act rationally if any opportunity offered itself. My compassion was another thing that I must control. It was compassion and temper that had me in my current mess, and neither had helped Charlie.

I returned my attention to my two companions. I appeared to be stuck with them.

The room remained quiet.

"Are you satisfied with what you do?" I asked Roy. "Do you want to be chained to Singh forever?"

"Some day he die," said Roy. "Then we free and horrors anybody we want, if we get away from Mrs. Singh and them."

"So why don't you kill him?" I asked. "You two are close enough to him, and he trusts you now. With that kind of surprise, Mrs. Singh wouldn't even know about it until you were well away."

"Too strong," said Roy. "Tried once. Couldn't get past he protection. He never even know I try. That how good he protection. He never even know."

A knock came at the door, then shouts and heavy pounding when there was no response.

"Should open it for they," Malcolm said with a grin. "See how they like that kind of answer to they knock."

There was a small but heated argument outside, and the door opened, admitting a group of three uniformed policemen. The first to enter took one look around and ran for the telephone. The others looked at the damaged door and wall, then moved across the room near Charlie's corpse.

The first policeman now had the phone and was starting to dial. Malcolm walked over and pulled the phone away. The guy almost fell.

"Don' damage they," said Roy. He looked at me. "Mr. Singh he not happy if we humbug without orders," he explained. "He don' say no this time, but he don' have problem any of these guys and them. Not right now. So we go easy."

"He no care if we do some *little* humbugging," Malcolm said, as he tripped the second policeman. "Little humbug can' hurt."

"Truth," answered Roy with a grin.

"Why?" I asked. "Why does he bother holding you back at all?"

Roy shrugged, not too interested. "Maybe other Obeah," he answered. "Don' know. He don' tell we and thing. None of we business I guess."

One of the police managed the telephone and was talking to someone excitedly. The others moved about carefully, as if afraid to touch anything. They appeared more cautious than fearful, despite the oddity of the scene. It was evident they had gone through this before and knew what was happening, but had no fear for their own safety at the moment. However, caution was the order of the day. Why be stupid.

Malcolm tripped one and sent him sprawling.

Roy giggled.

"I'm going to kill Singh," I said flatly, mainly to see what their reaction would be. Also, I meant it.

I blamed Singh for Charlie's death, not Malcolm or Roy. They were just the tools Singh used. Singh had made the decision, named the executioners, gave them detailed instructions on how to proceed, and, then, had calmly implemented his decision.

I wanted revenge.

That affair with the police only reminded me how corrupt Singh was. It reminded me to what lengths he was willing to go to satisfy personal peeves, reminded me how twisted his thinking was, how dangerous he was.

I wanted to be sure where these two stood; I wanted to know if they would try to stop me, if they were pro-Singh as a matter of habit or just through fear.

Malcolm laughed. "First you got to take he punish. By and by, you work for he, and you be happy, sort of. You going to see, man."

I hit my fist at the wall, heard the sound, and saw the startled look on one policeman's face. "Never happy," I said, "not around something like Singh. I want him dead, and I want to do it myself. Before, I just wanted free of this asshole, now I want his ass. He's not perfect. All these precautions he takes show he's scared shitless, that he knows he is vulnerable. Sooner or later he'll make a mistake, and when he does I'll have my chance."

"More like you end up in a bottle," said Roy.

"Are you going to tell him what I said?" I growled, whirling to face him. "Get me in more trouble? Be the protector of the great Singh? Chalk up some brownie points?"

"No," he answered, unperturbed. "We never tell anything unless he make we, or order ahead of time. Course you not first to decide to kill Mr. Singh."

"Better hope he leave you widow alone," added Malcolm.

I glared at him, ready to restart our fight.

"Hey, man, not me," he protested. "I talking 'bout Mr. Singh, man."

I relaxed, just a little. "If he touches her or has her touched, he can never trust me, because I'll get him for sure. No matter what happens to me."

Malcolm laughed. He knew I had cooled down, seemed to want me fired up again. "Big talk," he said. "Remember, he tell you, if you don' help, he go for she?"

"I helped," I answered. "I just couldn't kill my best friend. For that, somehow, I'm going to make him pay."

"He don' damage your lady," Roy interjected. "Not yet. So long as you work for he, so long as you of any use to he. That he leash. Malcolm trying to get you vex, wants you to do something stupid. That bullshit. That just get Mr. Singh vex. Don' worry on what happen widow. Right now she safe."

I sat back down, mollified. Nothing had changed, then, not yet. So long as I were useful, Jadine would be safe. Roy was right. Singh still had uses for me, for he could have had Fido tear me to pieces.

I might even get away with disobedience this once. At least, I hoped I would. The fact I was still in one piece was encouraging. However, next time Jadine could be in real danger.

The three policemen went outside, closing the door behind them. I had forgotten them completely. Malcolm reopened the door and left it standing open.

"Obeah, man," I heard one of the officers saying. "We wait outside." They did not reclose the door.

We sat quietly inside for another hour. My companions did not seem inclined to go outside. Photographers and other police personnel arrived, taking pictures, looking for other things. Malcolm and Roy tackled each group as they came, with no damage but lots of confusion. They did not allow me to slow down their fun with more conversation. I found myself thoroughly ignored for the moment. Eventually, no more police came. A panel van from a funeral home picked up the body.

I saw no signs of any Charlie spirit.

Time dragged.

Finally it was time for us to leave for our meeting with Singh. We left Charlie's place. It was full dark.

Resigned, I walked briskly with them. There was no point trying to run.

The trip did not seem so long this time, perhaps because of familiarity, perhaps I was numb from all that had happened. Whatever the reason, I saw the guttering of the Obeah flares with a touch of eagerness. I knew I was in for serious trouble, but at least I would be face-to-face with my tormenter.

Singh focused his eyes as we approached, the headless rooster pointing the way, as before. The head had to be somewhere, carefully arranged as always, but I didn't see it.

Does he raise all his roosters himself, I wondered.

I looked carefully at Singh. The daubing of blood on his body seemed less styled, more hurried. The dhoti was missing.

Had I managed to break his routine a little?

I wondered briefly how he decided on arrangements for his chickens, how he decided where to place the heads. Was it a set ritual, or did he just do it in whatever way appealed to him at the moment?

I kept looking for that chicken head, convinced its location was of prime importance to me. I had visions of the head in different spots, but never found it. My thoughts became more and more chaotic, nonsense ridden, almost panic-stricken.

I would like to see Singh look like his chicken, I thought. Fat chance. This guy is always ready for trouble. Walk softly and carry a big chicken.

I shivered, tried to firm up my mental shakes.

Singh grinned broadly. "Oh ho. My warriors return. I take it my friend, Mr. Emby, is no longer antagonistic."

"You bastard!" I growled.

"Ah, yes, the noble Mr. Correy," he said. "Malcolm had to use my pet to restrain you."

He held up a hand to silence me.

"Yes, Mr. Correy, I know all the details. The beast you call Fido is not stupid. I communicate quite comfortably with him, so I know all about the little fracas. You were very foolish, of course, but you are new. You will learn."

"Charlie was my friend," I told him.

"Yes, yes, of course. Wonderful thing, friendship. I trust you still plan to work for me."

The sarcasm dripped from his words.

I glowered at him.

"Come, come," he said. "I must have an answer."

"You have to leave Jadine alone," I snapped.

"Of course. You would be useless to me if she were not here. I thought this was understood. I keep forgetting the terrible ignorance of Americans in matters of the spirit world."

"Why did you kill Charlie?" I growled, my fists clenched. "He agreed to your terms."

Singh's face darkened. Fido moved up from the shadows, a rumble deep in his throat.

"You must not question my motives," he said. "This will be your only warning. Understood?" He watched me for a few seconds, took my silence for agreement, then continued. "You are not privileged to question me in any way. You are a spirit, and you are my property. You are a tool. If you do not function as I have decided you should, I will dispense with you, and with your leash. Is this all clear to you, Mr. Correy?"

I nodded, keeping a wary eye on Fido. I was not ready for that deep a confrontation. Maybe later, if I could figure how to survive the test, but not now.

"Very well," continued Singh. "Now to business. You were told to convince Mr. Emby. You tried and failed. You were told to help your companions terminate Mr. Emby. Instead, you attempted to stop them and fought with them. Also, when you first went to see Mr. Emby, you made an unauthorized side trip."

I moved closer, raised my hand. "Now wait—"

"No interruptions, please," he said, forestalling me. "I understand the problem over Mr. Emby's demise, and no harm was done by your interference, since he is now the late Mr. Emby. However, you dis-obeyed me by making that little trip to your widow, and you failed in your first assignment."

I looked at him. My disbelief at what I was hearing had to be obvious on my face, plain for him to read. What kind of values does this shithead have, I wondered.

He smiled. "As I said, I will disregard the interference matter this time," he continued, "but it must never happen again. I will not disregard the side trip and your failure in your assignment. Do you understand?"

"Yes," I answered.

He smiled again and gestured to Fido. Too late, I recognized what was happening and tried to run. Then Fido was on me.

CHAPTER SIXTEEN

My bout with Fido was very bad. This time, Singh made me impervious to permanent damage but not to pain. He wanted me to gain the full horror of Fido but remain intact for whatever Obeah work he had in mind. I did not even have the option of dying to escape the torture, for I was already dead. The fact that Singh combined my two punishments was no consolation at all.

After what seemed like hours, but, most likely, was only twenty or thirty minutes, Fido gave me one last shake and dropped me on the ground in front of Singh. The dog thing reverted to his normal size, his red eyes still glittering with excitement.

Singh let me lie there a few minutes and worry about whether it was over. Finally, he looked at me again, a hint of amusement in his eyes. "Please sit up, Mr. Correy," he said.

I did.

I was rather surprised that it was still possible after what I had been through. Slowly I became aware I had not been harmed permanently. I was in as good a shape as when this started, except for my memories. I continued to sit quietly, looking at Singh, wary.

"Very good," he said. "I trust you are now in a more receptive frame of mind."

I glared at him, until Fido growled again.

"Okay," I said, a little hurriedly, "so what's next on the agenda?"

"Much better," he said, softly. "First, a small discussion. In the future, if you ever interfere with my agents in any way whatsoever or if you ever refuse to do a job for me, no matter what your reasons, I will allow my pet to visit your widow and force you to watch. It will be a termination visit, and your widow will no longer be usable as a leash, for she will be very, very dead. Then I shall place you beneath the ocean in chains for a few years. Understood?"

I nodded, not trusting myself to speak.

He continued. "Now, if you ever fail in your appointed task again, I will allow Fido or one of his kind to do you some permanent damage. With the proper spells, everlasting impairment is possible. My pets are normally very careful, unless of course they become too excited."

The ten commandments of Singh's world, I thought. Does he always do this, or is this just for my benefit?

I looked for Roy and Malcolm and saw them to one side, throwing something into the water. I returned my gaze to Singh. He was waiting, seemingly not bothered by my momentary inattention.

"I trust you have no questions concerning my methods of punishment," he said.

"Pretty stiff," I answered.

I was a little amused. He had not said anything I had not heard from Roy and Malcolm, and somehow his dry delivery made it appear less real. Especially distracting was the way he kept scratching one foot with the other. Athlete's foot? I wondered.

"Be warned, Mr. Correy," he continued. You have had your slack time." He paused. Then, "I have decided to let you rest for three days at the cemetery, to allow you to become acquainted with my other staff. Please do not attempt to leave there before the three days are up. From now, you must always remember your time is no longer yours, it is mine."

He watched me carefully for a few seconds, as if making up his mind about something. "Enough on this," he said, finally. "At the end of the three days, Malcolm and Roy will escort you to your next employment. They will inform you of your duties in detail at that time, but, basically, your job will be to convince an American family to leave the country. The father has greatly displeased me, and I want him gone. I do not require you to harm him or his family, unless that is the only way they can be persuaded."

"Sounds simple enough," I replied, thankful the monologue was ending. "At least, no one is to be hurt this time."

"Unless they refuse to leave!" Singh snapped. "Roy and Malcolm will become a part of your team the instant it becomes apparent that the father has made the wrong decision."

"What do you mean by the word apparent?" I asked.

Singh looked at me smugly, a half-smile playing on his lips. "Do you remember the blue rash on your friend Mr. Emby?"

"Yeah," I answered.

Here it comes, I thought. Jadine and Isha had it pegged.

Singh watched my face. Satisfied with whatever he thought he saw, he resumed his conversation. "This is not an indication of Obeah interest as your Jadine no doubt told you. We who practice Obeah are aware of the rumors prevalent among the general population that the rash indicates interest by someone like me, and it suits our purpose to allow this misconception to continue."

He grinned. I was starting to hate that grin of his, but at least he wasn't digging at his feet now.

"Yes," he continued. "This sudden rash is a visual indication that the recipient of Obeah attention has decided to resist. So if either Roy or Malcolm should see such a rash, they know their assistance is required at once."

"So they knew all the time with Charlie," I said, finally. I shook my head. "They knew he had decided the wrong way before Charlie even told me."

Singh grinned, broadly, showing most of his teeth, obviously pleased by my reaction.

"Yes, indeed," he said. "I did not permit early action, however. I wished to see what your methods might accomplish."

"Shit," I growled. "You don't give a damn about methods. It was a test!"

"Suit yourself," purred Singh. "Now, back to my business. This particular family includes two children under the age of ten. You will attempt to convince the parents by way of dreams and wild manisfestations to prove your presence. If they resist, you will humbug the children, damaging if necessary, and let the parents know in advance what will happen. You will have two weeks to complete your persuasions. You know the penalties for failure or for disobedience."

I was still pissed over the blue rash business, but I knew better than to ignore him. "Yeah," I said. "You made that clear. Can I use my own tactics? So long as you don't see this blue shit?"

Singh laughed, delighted. "Oh ho! I perceive you are reluctant to damage children, Such compassion, so seldom seen among my staff. Very well. Use your own tactics. However, I honestly believe you will find the resistance of the adults to be less if the children are involved."

"Thank you," I replied. "Will these two obey my orders on this assignment? Will they keep their hands off unless I ask for help or they see your blue gunk?"

"Of course," he said, starting to become a little irritated. "I told you it's your job. I do hope you will perform better this time and not give me cause to be vexed again. I dislike punishment sessions."

He brooded silently in the glare of his Obeah torches for a short while, then looked up.

"Very well," he said, "be gone from me now. Malcolm and Roy will escort you to the cemetery."

There was no choice. We left.

*   *   *

I worried about the new assignment on our long trip back. There was no question of refusal. To me, the family's upheaval and move from Trinidad was insignificant compared to the havoc for me and Jadine if I were to refuse the job. In any event, refusal would only cause Singh to use someone else.

Singh had capitulated on the question of violence to the children. I could only hope that in future he would permit me to avoid senseless violence provided I could give him the results he desired.

"An American family," he had said. Most likely none of them believed in ghosts or Obeah, and they would be completely unprepared for what was about to happen to them.

I only hoped they would not decide to fight, as Charlie had.

Charlie, I thought. How about Charlie? I wondered if that had been him at his house, before the police got there, and what he must have thought as he recovered his senses. I remembered being very confused.

I wondered how long it would be before I could contact him. I could use that brain of his right now. He had a mind like a steel trap. It was never his smarts that got him in trouble, it was his stubborn streak.

I remembered Charlie telling me he planned on being buried in Trinidad, so he would be stuck here now, and vulnerable to Singh like me.

A violent death supposedly brought strength to a spirit, but it took so long to get that strength organized that someone like Singh can get through long before the spirit can effectively resist. It also appeared that Singh ordered death when he planned to use the spirit later. If true, it might well mean Charlie was being set up to be my partner. Strength won't help Charlie against someone like Singh. If Singh planned this, there was little Charlie could do.

All in all, it was becoming probable that Charlie would be no help to me at all, and he would end up like me. Except, maybe, Malcolm and Roy could get me to this Marion Fields, and she could help me get Charlie organized before Singh did.

Wishful thinking. I tried to keep the swirling thoughts down, not wanting to raise my hopes at all. Me getting the big rebellion organized, that was the blind leading the blind for truth.

I watched Malcolm and Roy. They were not very talkative on that monotonous journey back to St. James, back to the Western Cemetery, and that was completely unlike these two. Generally they had diarrhea of the mouth.

Looking at them, I had some idea what I might expect when I reached the cemetery, so far as Singh's staff was concerned. My presumption was that any spirit I met that was staff would bear visible deformities or injuries attesting to their *softening up* or miscellaneous punishments. I was not sure if Singh's actions were typical of his breed, but I suspected that to be the case.

I wasn't sure how Singh's spirits could be distinguished from those belonging to some other Obeah man, or if it made any difference. Of course, some deformities could be from particularly nasty deaths.

I wondered about the pets Singh had said were watching the cemetery exits. I decided to ask one of my companions, choosing Malcolm as he had always appeared to be more willing to talk. So I asked.

"Not like Fido," he answered. "More like big bird with claws and thing. Like vultures, maybe. Look very nasty, but don' hurt. Least don' hurt we in cemetery. Never tangle with one away from there. Maybe bad like Fido, but don' know. They belong Singh, so probably real nasty."

He seemed to warm to his subject. "Sometimes Mr. Singh he take some of they away to work for he and thing. Usually they stay with we at cemetery. Six of they, all alike. Huge, black, stare at you like they hungry. Never make a sound."

"What's it like in the cemetery?" I asked. "You and Roy are the only spirits I've seen since I died."

"Lots of we, man," he said. "You just don' run across. Not so many like live people. After while, some move into they coffin and thing, gone then, but still plenty. Stronger spirits stay longer, the bad guys and the ones that die hard." He shrugged. "The good ones get lost, man. They gone."

"Some life," I muttered.

"You not alive. Different rules now," he said.

They both laughed. We continued.

We passed Cocorite. Malcolm and Roy had a brief argument over whether to do some quick humbugging in that crowded village, then they decided it was not worth the punishment they would almost certainly receive.

We kept on into St. James and into the cemetery. The place was not large, about two or three blocks deep and two wide, almost a square, with that low, white block wall around it. There were two entrances, actually just stone columns with wrought iron gates.

It did not have to be large, I remembered. Often other bodies were buried above the original bodies, making more efficient use of the available space. Jadine had told me about this. I had made it a point, when buying my plot, to be sure that it was only the ones who didn't buy their spaces that got bodies on top of them.

"Do we have to stay by our graves?" I asked.

It was Roy who answered. "Go anywhere," he said. "Just don' leave cemetery. This not licks and thing. Big-time social hour. Better you meet others, like Mr. Singh say."

"Yeah," Malcolm added. "Mr. Singh he want you be all social now, make friends, be civilized. Be a little ghost with culture, be a good boy."

"Yeah," I said. "Sounds like fun."

"Suit yourself," said Roy

He and Malcolm sauntered off.

I wandered around, bored. I took a good look at Singh's bird pets. They were real monstrocities, almost as big as men with tiny heads and large, taloned feet. They were huge, black vulture-like creatures. They glared at me hungrily with unwinking red eyes. I left them alone.

I met several ghosts, maybe with Singh and maybe not. I did not ask.

Some looked like normal people, others were badly mutilated. None paid much attention to me. Most just walked about, muttering to themselves.

I assumed those that were mutilated belonged to either Singh or some other Obeah man. I might have asked, but I didn't want to get involved to that extent. I had the feeling that if I got down to mixing with these spirits on a social level I would be like them.

Occasionally someone talked to me. Sometimes I answered, sometimes not. I tried to find Charlie. I looked for Marion.

I found Charlie's grave, but he wasn't there, probably had no desire to be there. I remembered I had not been the least interested in staying at this place, and I still felt the same. Some spirit told me Marion was on a job or something like that. It did not sound encouraging. She might be as bad as Roy or Malcolm. I still planned to talk to her, but I would not get my hopes up, again.

Several times I looked up Malcolm or Roy, and once I met someone I knew when I was alive. Again no help. He was not involved with Singh, but he was so confused it was difficult to talk to him.

The time passed, slowly.

The only excitement came on the second night when two boys invaded the cemetery, on a dare.

They were American boys, of course. No Trinidad boy would dream of entering a cemetery at night, especially with a full moon riding the night sky. The local boys knew better. So did these boys, but a dare is a very big thing for a boy of any age.

The word zipped through the quiet cemetery like a prairie fire. Little happened here to ease the boredom, and, when something finally did, they were always ready. Since this cemetery seemed to be a holding pen for Singh's staff, or staff for other Obeah masters, the intense interest generated by someone entering the grounds quickly degenerated to an eagerness to frighten, to haunt or humbug. If someone were foolish enough to intrude, then they were fair game.

The boys, about fourteen or fifteen years in age, apparently only planned to walk from one side of the cemetery to the other. At least, that was the word circulating.

The various shades were stumbling over each other in their eagerness but still allowed the boys to pass the halfway mark without bothering them in any way. It was the largest grouping of spirits I had seen since my death.

Finally, unable to restrain himself any longer, a red-haired, Rasta half-breed pushed over a tombstone directly in front of one boy, almost hitting him.

The boy fell to the ground avoiding the stone, and both of them screeched in fear.

A female spirit, with half her face and breasts eaten away, moved to the front. She was also missing part of a foot, but it didn't appear to bother her.

The redhead moved out of her way. "Do your thing, Marion," he said.

I stared at her. My God, I thought, it's Charlie's Marion. She was no longer the girl I remembered, not the same girl that Charlie had known.

I had not recognized her at all. I had not known her well, but the changes were appalling. She had only been dead a year, but she was almost unrecognizable. To me, it was the most encouraging sight I had seen since I died. These multiple mutilations were a clear sign she had done some heavy rebelling against Singh. She should be receptive to anything that might get rid of Singh.

She seemed to be a nervous bundle of energy, and she had a manic look on her ravaged face. She moved quickly to the two boys and stopped briefly as one of them tried to pull the other to his feet.

Before he was fully up, she had his pants off and thrown to one side. It was clear that neither boy had seen her or any others. The pants were gone, though, and there was a feeling of excitement in the air that I could sense from where I stood.

"Josh, something's playing with my prick!"

Josh had already seen, for now the jockey shorts had been ripped off, and his friend appeared to be moving forward without moving his feet, his sex stretched in front as if he were being pulled forward by something using that as a handle. It was Marion pulling him. I saw her plainly. To the boys, the cemetery was empty.

Sight was not needed for what was happening to him.

"Josh, help me! Something's got me!"

Josh tried. He pulled on his friend's arm, attempting to stop him. Now another spirit had Josh's fly open, and had her hand inside fondling the balls.

"Can't help you, Brad," he grunted. "You got to pull loose. They're after me, too."

There was a big commotion, and I couldn't see what happened next. Too many spirits around the boys.

"C'mon, let's get outa here," screamed Brad, finally breaking free of the circle.

Josh broke loose, also, naked, and they both ran back the way they had come in. Despite his self-evident fear, Josh had a very obvious erection, and I could see Marion running beside him playing him off as they ran.

Her handicaps were not slowing her at all. Since Roy and Malcolm knew her, she must belong to Singh. If all her scars and deformities were because of disobedience, Singh must have his hands full with this one.

The cemetery was not large, but the kids probably felt it was huge, for it took them a long time to reach the exit. When they reached the gate, they were being harassed by, at least, five spirits. Both were naked, and scratches and welts were easily visible.

They climbed over the wall next to the gate to save a few feet. The cemetery inhabitants let them go. They had only been after entertainment, although the boys had not known that.

Josh and Brad ran down the road, yelling, running as if chased by the devil himself.

The cemetery returned to its former peaceful state. I had stood there, as if hypnotized, watching the whole scene. I had felt no urge to join the fun, but it had been a fun thing. There had never been any intention to hurt the boys. The spirits started dispersing.

I moved forward, wanting to intercept Marion. I caught her eye, and she stopped and stared at me, recognition in her look. Then, without warning, she turned and ran.

I hunted, but to no avail.

Boredom returned.

I was almost thankful, on the third night, when Malcolm and Roy came to collect me for my next job.

CHAPTER SEVENTEEN

The Bronson family lived in Maraval, in a neighborhood predominantly populated by expatriate Americans. James and Lindsey Bronson were a handsome couple, James about thirty-one or two, Lindsey maybe twenty-nine. Their children were beautiful, blonde like their parents, and loving. Tony was nine and Cindy no more than seven.

I liked them at once.

Jim Bronson was an engineer, but what his connection with Singh might be I could not tell. They seemed to live a quiet life and had no obvious intention of remaining in Trinidad after Bronson's contract expired in 1982. It was a good family, a loving one. The information poured in as we walked around, listened, rustled through papers. Then the Bronsons went to bed and the house darkened.

I felt sick. I don't want to hurt them, I thought. They're good people.

Nothing had changed. I thought of Jadine and my own three small children and knew I had no choice. I had to convince them to move, to get the hell out of Trinidad, to get out now.

I walked around the darkened house, with Malcolm and Roy right behind me. I wanted to get the feel of it.

It was ranch-style, with three bedrooms. The children used one, the parents another; the extra bedroom was occupied by a live-in maid, named Jessi, a black girl of maybe twenty or so who helped Lindsey manage the house and children. The house had a large, kitchen-dining room, an even larger front room, and a study. A new Escort, furnished as part of Jim's contract, was parked in an attached garage next to the kitchen. Jim's company owned the house.

The children and Jessi became restless when we paused in their rooms. The parents slept soundly, undisturbed. A large German shepherd slept on a mat outside, his face toward the gate at the end of the driveway. His lips pulled back in a sudden snarl as we passed near him. He did not wake.

Malcolm grinned at the dog's silent snarl, looked over at me. "We start now?" he asked, eagerly.

I turned on him, remembering Charlie, recalling how that one had started easy and then soured. I did not want this one to go the same way, and these two were already so bored they couldn't see straight. Even knowing how dangerous it was, I couldn't keep my own frustration from surfacing, my fears.

"We start when I say," I snapped, "and we do it my way. Okay?"

I was very nervous, very uneasy. I had gone from believing Singh was a clown, then thinking he might be omnipotent, and finally felt he could be vulnerable. In any event, I did not need to get these two all pissed off this early in the job. I calmed myself, then turned back to Malcolm.

"Sorry," I said, meaning it. "Didn't intend to snap at you."

He shrugged. "No fun, this one."

"I hope not," I answered. "Before I do anything, I want to watch these people and see how they live. Then I'll know how to proceed."

"Best way just give some quick horrors early, then let they know what's going on," said Roy.

"That's your way, not mine." I reviewed what I had learned so far, mentally, wanting to be sure I had seen everything. "I want to do things a little slower," I insisted. "I don't want to screw it up. Let's take one more look."

We moved back through the house, back to where we had entered, passing through the same rooms again, taking a quick second look. After Charlie, I was gun shy.

The children had settled back into deep sleep, Cindy hugging a large teddy bear tightly. Jessi was still restless. The older Bronsons were entwined loosely on their bed, the covers thrown free, cooled by a large fan. There was no air conditioning in use, although a unit was in the window. Their door was closed, to keep the children from bursting in on them in the night, but not locked. The closed door was no hindrance.

"I bigger than he," said Malcolm proudly.

"Doesn't do you much good," I retorted.

Roy grinned.

We moved on.

After the house, we spent the rest of the night checking the surrounding neighborhood. There was no real reason for it except Roy said they did it so they would know the escape routes. Escape routes for the victims, not us.

The next morning started early. Jim left for work in Tacarigua at shortly after six, and his wife rose with him.

Jessi woke soon afterwards and started wheedling the children into their school uniforms, then to their breakfast table. They left for their private school by maxi-taxi shortly before eight.

That evening, Jim Bronson worked in his study for an hour or so, then joined his family and Jessi to watch television, a video movie which I found interesting. By ten they were all in bed except Jessi, who watched a late movie. The children soon were asleep, and the Bronsons talked idly in bed, preparing to make love.

"We start now?" asked Malcolm for the third time that day.

He was extremely bored. I knew this boredom might develop into mischief later, and I knew I would have to find some way they could help. Otherwise they might mess things up just to have something to do. As of now, I didn't see any way they could help without making matters worse. I would have to do something, though, or I would soon have a rebellion on my hands.

"I start tonight, once they're asleep," I said. "Sorry, but if I get through you won't have anything to do. If I don't make any progress, I will try to come up with a way to use you guys. I'm not trying to keep you out of it just for the hell of it. I simply fail to see where your methods will help."

"You have to convince they that dream is real and thing," said Roy. Very low key. I guess he wanted to avoid getting me nervous or angry.

"No big deal." I was still standing in the bedroom. "I didn't have any trouble with Charlie," I continued. "That doesn't take any partic-ular talent. Look, let me think about it. Meantime, stick around if you want. I have nothing to hide, and I may still find something."

I sat down in a stuffed chair in the bedroom, waiting for the Bronsons to go to sleep, which looked to be some time off. They were making love energetically, with considerable imagination.

"Don' like to watch they," said Roy.

"Why?" I asked. "Because you can't do anything since you died?"

"Still can, in dream world, but you no let we in there yet." Roy was standing near the door. "That part of the fun on these jobs. We can do a lot of things in dream without damaging the target."

"Do it on your own jobs," I said. "Not on mine."

"Screw you, Clark!" growled Roy. He left to watch the movie showing in the front room.

"How about you?" I asked Malcolm, curious.

"Don' mind watching," he answered. In fact, he was standing near the bed and would find it hard to miss any of what was going on.

"Sorry, I can't use you guys," I said. "Maybe later."

"That's okay, man." He was watching me now instead of the Bronsons. "Mr. Singh, he say do it your way, so we do it your way. But we could help."

"How?" I asked. I stayed in my chair. I saw no reason not to be comfortable.

Malcolm said, "If you let we help, it go easier for you if you fail. Can' hurt. We do our part like you tell we. No more, no less. That way we get to do something, and you plans don' get screwed. I tell you man, we just sit around and Roy going to climb walls and thing. And same thing maybe me. I bet you find we help not so bad."

I thought about that, including the implied threat. I might mess this job up more by keeping these two away from it than if I just gave in and let them help me. At least, I might be able to keep some control.

"All right," I said. "That sounds reasonable. I might as well let you earn your keep."

I paused for a short time, thinking. I wanted to do this right. "Listen, then," I said. "I'll visit the parents tonight. You and Roy can get into Jessi's dreams. Nothing physical, the dreams only. I want you to try to get her to quit. My job will be easier if she's gone. I want these people to be dependent only on themselves."

Malcolm grinned. "Right, Captain. I tell Roy."

He left the room, obviously in a good mood.

Briefly, I thought of backing out, but I let it stand. To back out now would cause serious trouble, and it sure as hell would do no harm to have their backing if I screwed up. They would give Jessi some bad nightmares, but it would not harm her physically. Sooner or later she would awaken, no worse for her experience.

Malcolm came back in. "She asleep, on couch with television on and thing. We going in now. Want to watch we, or you going to keep watching they screw?"

It sounded interesting, so I stood to join them. "Remember," I said. "Don't hurt her. Just nightmare stuff."

"Yeah," he grinned, "and we tell she to leave. 'Member, you leave we alone, let we have our fun. We get our kicks, she remember nightmare. Okay?"

I shrugged. "Why not."

They were both grinning now, almost dancing in their eagerness.

"Now you see pro in action," said Malcolm. "See how it done, man."

"No objections," I said. "Go ahead. This is the only thing I've seen in Singh's world that can be enjoyed freely, without hurting someone."

Roy laughed. "You hung up on that, man. Too much feelings for strangers and them. You wake up soon, you betcha."

All three of us went into Jessi's dream at the same time. The television droned on, unwatched. We found her on her own bed in her dream. She was nude, and was undressing a young man I assumed was her boyfriend.

We watched for a few seconds.

"Don' forget," said Malcolm, "you say this one is we own."

I grinned. "I remember. Go ahead. Maybe I'll learn something."

Malcolm laughed, almost a giggle. He and Roy both dispensed with their clothes. I took a good look and decided that Malcolm was indeed better equipped than Bronson. I watched as the two of them moved to the dream couple and stood over them. The couple on the bed were much too busy to notice them.

Roy giggled, a silly sound, but it caught Jessi's attention. She looked up, her eyes widened.

The boyfriend pumped away, undisturbed.

Roy reached out one hand and lifted the boyfriend away from Jessi, then strangled him while Malcolm held Jessi and made her watch, laughing softly all the time. The boy-friend vanished, and Malcolm turned Jessi to face him.

He stuffed his huge tool into her mouth and then, ignoring the strangled screams, screwed her mouth. Meanwhile, Roy had entered her from the back.

Disgusted, I turned away.

I wasn't disgusted with what they were doing *per se*. I mean, different strokes for different folks. What bugged me was the violence, the cruelty. Perhaps they wanted shock value, but I doubted they needed so heavy a hand.

Finally they had enough and sat her down to talk. They told her she had to quit her job and that they would kill her if she did not. They made dream images to show the many ways they might choose to do it.

Then, Malcolm promised her that he would give proof they were really there when she woke. He looked at me, and I nodded. I had allowed this much; I had to allow the proof, or the whole thing was pointless. From what I had seen, this dream was sure to have an effect on her. Being a Trinidadian, she would know she had been "humbugged" or "haunted." On that she would have no doubt.

They told her to wake, and we moved from the dream. Jessi woke suddenly, sat up straight on the couch, her eyes wide, and sobbed softly. Malcolm turned off the television, and her eyes became a little wild. Roy squeezed one breast rhythmically while Malcolm ran a hand up and down beneath her house dress. Then they stood back and let her run, stumbling and crying, into her room.

We were quiet for a few minutes. They both looked smug, satisfied with their efforts, but I was pensive. Still, there was nothing I could say, no quarrel I could pick. They had done as they had said they would.

No more, no less.

They had kept their word, and there was no way I could complain.

"See how it work?" asked Malcolm. "Now it your turn with parents and them. Should be asleep by now."

"Yeah," I said. "Now it's my turn."

* * *

Roy and Malcolm wanted to join me. I said no.

I wanted to use the soft sell on the first contact, not the rough approach. I knew they might do more than just observe, so I did not want my methods circumvented before I could apply them. I was aware I might eventually do things I did not like in the Bronson dream worlds, but I had no intention of being too pushy early. I was almost certain I never would be tempted to go to the extremes used by my companions.

However, after Maharaj, I did have a few doubts. In this particular case, Singh was aware of the value of a civilized approach, and that's why he had me in charge despite my screwup with Charlie.

I would have to be more forceful in this dream medium than I ever was in life, for people ignored or forgot dreams which were tame or ordinary, and I was a stranger to this family. I hated like hell to admit it, but Roy and Malcolm might have the right approach for this medium of communication.

I had hit Maharaj hard in his dreams, and got results. I had gone easy with Charlie, and he was dead.

I approached Jim Bronson first, because he was dreaming at the moment, and his wife was not. I was not particular.

He was in a snowstorm, driving, somewhere in upstate New York. I entered as a hitchhiker, joining him in the front seat of his car, shivering. He was alone and looked younger, somehow. I wondered if he were having a dream about a time before he got married.

No matter, I gave him car trouble, and he pulled over to one side. Then I banished the snowstorm and the car and transferred us to a park bench in the sun where we could talk.

"Who the hell are you?" he asked. His tone of voice was conversational. People are never surprised at anything that turns up in their dreams, even when it's completely out of their experience.

Jim was comfortable. He thought he was in control. He knew I was something alien, for he had never met me in real life. However, it was his dream.

He turned a little to face me fully. "I asked you who the hell you were," he repeated.

"You don't know me," I said, "but I made sure Jessi will quit in the morning. That will be the start of a lot of problems for you if you don't do exactly what I tell you to do."

I thought he was going to wake up right then and there, from disgust. "This has to be a dream," he growled.

"Yeah," I answered. "This is a dream, but this dream is real." As I talked I became more and more agitated. I was getting fed up with being told I didn't exist. "My name is Clark Correy," I continued. "I died last year. Check the records. You'll find me there. Car accident. Left a pregnant widow and two kids. It's all easy to verify, simple. When the maid quits, you'll know you'd better review everything I tell you. You sure as hell better check me out."

I was starting to enjoy the encounter, despite myself. My irritation left as I settled into my purpose. Just for fun I created a second park bench, got up and sat there, facing him.

He blinked, but said nothing.

"You want another name?" I asked. "Try Charles Emby, American. He died four days ago, along with his girl friend, Isha. Very messy, very bloody. Police have no idea what happened. I was there, I saw it happen. It was a couple of these non-existent ghosts. They killed the two of them, and did it with terrible cruelty. You can check Charles Emby. It's in the papers, the Guardian."

"What do you want from me?" he asked. The confusion I had noted earlier was no longer evident in his speech. He was adjusting to my presence. I wondered if this were good or bad.

"You and your family must leave Trinidad," I said.

"Sure. Next year. End of my contract." It was a quick answer, no hesitation.

"No, in two weeks," I said. "No later." I made my answer as short and definite as his response had been.

"You're out of your mind." He got off the bench and started pacing. I banished the bench. Let him walk or stand, I thought.

I remained seated, comfortable.

"No choice, Jim," I said. "You pissed off the wrong people here, and they want you gone. Right now. If you don't leave, they can get very nasty, and someone could get hurt, even killed. You or one of your family."

"Now, wait a minute!" he yelled. No more easy conversational tone. Now things were serious. I didn't like what I was doing, but I had to get through to him quickly. This was one way to do it. I knew he would not be easy to convince, and I had already seen the light touch was not working.

If I need to, I thought, I'll bring in Malcolm and Roy. Whatever it takes.

Jim was glaring, his fists clenched. "Listen, asshole! You are way the hell off base now. Dream or no dream."

"No time, Jim," I said. "I'm not kidding, and I don't have time to be gentle. Like it or not, you have no choice."

"I couldn't leave in two weeks if I had to." he answered, "and I do not appreciate threats to my family."

Now he's listening, I thought. Maybe I can get through now.

"Listen," I snapped.

He stopped pacing and stood and glared at me.

"That's better," I said. "I'm not sorry about the threats, as I meant every word. If I don't do it, someone else will. Those threats are promises. You and your family are at risk. You must leave this country, and there is no way out of that."

I felt like pacing now, to offset my increasing nervousness. I remained seated, tried to look calm. "Look at me, Jim. Pay attention. These Obeah people don't play games. If you don't leave, you're going to be haunted in the worst sense of the word. It's no joke, and it is happening, right now. And it is happening to you."

Am I getting through? I wondered. Bastard has a poker face.

"My work, my contract," he sputtered, finally.

"They'll have to go," I said. "Your life is more important."

"I don't believe this shit," he growled, anger starting to appear in his voice. "Even if it were true, I don't believe you can do what you say."

"Remember, I told you Jessi will quit tomorrow," I said. I had started this conversation with that same information. Maybe he would listen this time.

"Terrorized in her sleep no doubt," he growled. "That won't carry over. She hasn't been hurt, or her yells would have me woke by now."

"No, not hurt," I answered, getting a little irritated, myself. He still stood, pacing now and then. I did not replace his park bench. I tried to look comfortable. "She did get proof that something was here in the night," I said. "something that visited you and her and your wife. Ask her."

I concentrated, made him stop pacing. Startled, he looked at me.

"Jim," I said. "Don't get the idea in your head that I can't hurt you, and don't rely too heavily on my statement that I don't want to hurt you. If you refuse to listen, or make the wrong decision, I will be forced to do something. If my companions join me it could be very bad."

He did not react, did not move.

I shrugged, continued. "Bad dreams may not be enough to force you out of the country, but a few demonstrations tomorrow will show you I can affect much more than dreams. I'll keep it small, as I don't want to hurt anyone if I can avoid it, but I will do whatever is needed."

"I still don't believe in you," he said.

I found I was now getting more than a little irritated, and very frustrated. What does it take to get through to this clown? I wondered.

I tried again. "You will," I answered, trying to stay reasonable. "I will convince you, as soon as you wake up. Tomorrow, you will have no doubt I am real. At the moment I'm limited to this dream, but it would be wise for you to pay very close attention to me. I'm not like your tame, ordinary, run-of-the-mill dreams, Jim. When you wake up I'll still be around. And I bite."

He appeared to be listening. I relented, gave him back his park bench. Gratefully, he sat, not once taking his eyes off me.

"Okay," I said. "Check with my wife, Jadine. She will tell you what happened to me, and to my friend Charles Emby. Get the date from my wife, and you can read about Charlie in the *Guardian*. Get a copy if you don't still have one lying around."

I paused, tried to gauge my effect on him. "Better listen up, Jim," I said. "I'm bad news, but my friends are worse. You're not in America now. This is Trinidad, and you made somebody mad. Now it's payback time!"

What the hell, I thought. I have to hit him hard, right from the start. I must not hold back.

"This country is heavy in Obeah, Jim," I continued. "You know, like VooDoo. Obeah likes kids. Children are so vulnerable, and all children believe in ghosts. Obeah can do nasty things to children."

With that, I left his dream. With those last words about children, I saw his face go white. That got through, even in the dream. With all my arguments, all my talking, the only time I seemed to get through was when I was talking about the kids.

I shivered, appalled. No way, Singh, I thought. I don't hurt kids.

*   *   *

I watched Lindsey and waited until I was sure she was dreaming, then I entered her dream.

She was involved in some kind of picnic or barbecue in their back yard, complete with Jim, the children, and ants. She and Jim were on lawn chairs, and the children were running around the area.

I banished everything but Lindsey herself. I sat near her, taking Jim's chair, and made her look at me. She was not surprised, just curious. The usual dream reaction.

"Do I know you?" she asked.

"No. I'm a ghost."

She frowned. "That's a funny thing to say. I must be dreaming. People only talk like that in dreams."

Here we go again, I thought. Mentally, I groaned. As soon as someone says "I'm dreaming", they don't believe a single thing you say unless you club them over the head with it.

Resigned, I held my temper, and kept my voice reasonable. "Yes, you're dreaming," I said, "but I am not a dream. I'm real. You'll know that in the morning when you find out your husband also dreamed about me, and when Jessi quits."

"Jessi? Quit? Over a dream? Why should she?" She frowned and looked a little indignant. "We've always treated Jessi good, like one of the family, and the kids would be devastated if she quit. No, she wouldn't just quit, not without more reason than a silly damn dream."

I stopped her tirade by taking her chin in my hand and turning her head back to face me again. She had started looking for Jim or the kids.

"Listen to me," I said. "Two friends of mine paid Jessi a visit in her sleep tonight and convinced her they were authentic. These friends were very nasty and not very subtle."

"What do you want?" she asked. I seemed to have her full attention now.

"I want you to convince your husband that all of you must leave Trinidad, within the next two weeks," I said.

She stared at me. I did nothing. I knew this time she was thinking about it.

Finally, "I can't do that. He has a contract. He is very conscientious about these things. He won't break his contract just because I give him pressure."

"He'll have to break it," I insisted. "Every one of you is in deadly danger. Your husband made somebody mad, somebody involved in Obeah." I paused and thought for a few seconds.

"Are you familiar with the term Obeah?" I asked. "It is like the very worst kind of VooDoo, and, if things get out of hand, someone could be hurt badly, or killed. I was sent by an Obeah man to convince you to leave, and the two friends I mentioned earlier came to help me. I prefer to do this by persuasion, but they will use violence."

I paused once more, trying to gauge her interest. Was it more or less? There was a peculiar look in her eyes, maybe curiosity. I couldn't tell if the curiosity was concerned with my story or with me.

Stubbornly, I continued. "I don't intend to fail. That would also bring penalties my way. Possibly you don't accept that or don't mind, but I do. My last punishment was quite unpleasant and did not leave my body in good condition."

I stopped completely, took her hand and pulled her to a standing position. "Take a look," I said.

I made my clothes vanish, except for my jockey shorts, then I shrugged and let them go, too. I wanted her to see the marks Fido left on me, and some were down low. The look of horror and disgust were as I hoped when she stared at my mutilations. I made myself some short pants. I wanted no distractions.

"You can be sure," I said, "that I don't wish for more scars. You can also be certain I will do almost anything to avoid them."

I was getting tired of talking. I set images of Malcolm and Roy in the yard, dressed as they were for Jessi's dream. I didn't say anything, just let her see them, let her make the connection.

"The whole thing is simple," I continued. "This man wants your husband and his family gone, and I need your help to be sure this happens.

Failure on my part would irritate him. When he gets irritated, his usual response is to arrange for torture, mutilation, and death." I pointed to Malcolm and Roy. "Two of his favorite convincers," I continued.

She was staring at the images I had made. I could see she was starting to comprehend what was happening.

I felt compassion but did not let that stop me. "Incidentally," I said, adding to the pressure, "he suggested I concentrate my efforts on your children."

"Tony and Cindy?" she cried in alarm, tearing her eyes off Malcolm and Roy.

Enough, I thought, and I made them vanish. I returned my attention to Lindsey. She had pulled away from me and kept repeating her kids' names.

"Unless I have the wrong family," I growled, finally. "Come on, lady, don't be dense. Of course I mean Tony and Cindy."

"Jim says dreams aren't real and neither are ghosts." She appeared angry. Good, I thought. Much better than panic.

"Better make your own decision about that," I said. "Your lives may be at stake."

"I thought these things never happened to real people," she said.

"They do," I answered. "You've been lucky. All your luck ran out here in Trinidad, though. Now, back to business, lady. You have to tell Jim to check all the people I told him about. I gave him several names: Correy, Emby, Isha. It's important that both of you satisfy yourselves that these people are real, and that what I have told you is the truth. Also talk to Jadine, my wife. She can confirm this too. Don't forget."

The landscape wavered, got a little fuzzy. Her dress fell off. "Can it be negotiated?" she asked, her voice hoarse, licking her lips as she looked at my Fido marks.

I grinned. Now it's getting interesting, I thought. These dreams are completely ass-end, over-backwards, unpredictable.

"No," I answered. "It can't be negotiated, but I think I might enjoy a deeper discussion."

She started to move back, changing her mind at the last minute, but I moved forward quickly. I pushed her to a lying position, a little roughly.

The scene that followed got rougher yet. I was tired of being reasonable, and I was horny as hell. So I screwed her, rough, and I did a few things impossible in real life, and some more that surprised her. She enjoyed it as much as I did.

Then, without another word, I left her dream world and started to leave her room.

"Any luck?" asked Malcolm. He and Roy had come in the bedroom while I was still in Lindsey's dream. I wasn't surprised. A little irritated, and possibly a little alarmed, but not surprised.

"Maybe," I answered, carefully. "I'll give them some calling cards when they get up, then let them think about their dreams during the day after they have their proof and know they all had interconnected dreams."

"Hope they turn you down," said Malcolm. "More fun the hard way. Lot more fun."

"You had fun with Jessi," I pointed out.

They both grinned, remembering.

"More fun when out of dream world," said Roy. "Can' screw then, but can give horrors to actual people. At least it mean something then, for we and they. We know it real, and they sure as hell know it real. Sometimes they forget dreams. They don' forget the horrors."

I did not bother answering. On the face of it, it did not seem to deserve a reply. However, I had changed a lot since my death. I had a different mind set about a lot of things. I did not want them to realize how much I agreed with Roy.

CHAPTER EIGHTEEN

Jessi quit the next morning.

She rose, packed her few things in her old, battered suitcase and departed without bothering about the few days' pay she had coming. She was from Trinidad, and protests from an American family meant nothing, for she knew how little they knew. She knew the signs, and she left.

After she was gone, her story of nightmares and Obeah still fresh in their ears, Jim and Lindsey looked at each other, knowing what was going to happen, neither wanting to start it.

Finally Lindsey could stand the silence no longer. She looked straight at Jim, her eyes wide. "I had a dream last night, too," she said. "About somebody who called himself Correy."

Jim looked haggard, his expression clearly saying he knew what she was going to say.

"Wait until the children leave," he said. He then left the room to get ready for work.

The kids left, after the customary hassle. The maxi-taxi collected them, absorbed their frantic energy, and carried them off to school.

The parents sat looking at each other for a while, reluctant.

Time's up, I thought.

I turned off the lights, turned them on again, turned on the stereo and put it on loud, moved an ashtray close to Jim's elbow from where it had rested on a different table, took the cigarette package from his pocket and dropped the cigarettes, one by one, in the ashtray. I took his lit cigarette from his mouth and put it out and then broke three of those already in the ashtray in half. Finally, I removed one ear ring from Lindsey's ear and dropped it in the same ashtray.

"Jim, what's going on?" asked Lindsey, in a voice that shook. "I don't think I want to stay here any longer. I want to go home, Jim."

"What was in your dream, hon?" His voice was quiet. He led her to the front room, and they both sat on the couch, quite close. He waited.

She told him, with some editing of the last part, but I didn't mind that. The sexual fun and games had nothing to do with the basic ideas

I wanted her to relate.

He stared at her, and then told her about his own dream and the names I had given him.

Lindsey looked even more scared now. She put one hand on his shoulder, squeezed on the muscle. "Jim, this is too real. This is scary. We've got to get out of here, we've got to leave."

Jim winced, moved her hand. "It's not that easy, honey. Contracts are not easy to break, and you need to be damn sure of yourself when you try to get out of one. Now, I agree something happened here, and maybe these tales of Obeah or VooDoo are based on some sort of fact. However, that won't help us out of a contract. Maybe we should be looking for a way to fight this stuff, instead. There has to be a way to fight back, and maybe that will be easier than the contract business."

Lindsey was losing some of the frightened look. Now she was starting to get worried, and a little angry. "Jim, didn't you hear Jessi's story? Or mine?"

"Yeah," he answered. "It was bad, but it was a dream. Listen, honey, I'll check around, see if I can come up with something."

She jumped to her feet. "We can't take the chance," she shouted. "We have two kids. We have to watch out for them."

He groaned and followed her across the room. "We can't just go, honey. If I leave now, I lose my job. We'll be on unemployment back in the States, and the terms of my contract say I'll have to pay for our move back if I break the agreement. It would gobble up half our savings, maybe more. Then I'll play hell getting the next job, maybe even lose out on unemployment since they could call it leaving without good cause. They could even sue me."

"But, Jim," she protested.

"No *buts*," he answered. The firmer tone in his voice stopped her. "I have to check it out, but I will make sure our tax visas are up-to-date. Okay? Is that enough for what's scaring you. I'll investigate on the one hand, to see if anything can be done, but I'll make the paperwork preparations for leaving as well."

She thought about that, studied it. She moved back to the couch, sat, and put her head in her hands for a minute. Finally, "All right, Jim. You handle it, but don't ignore it. We're all involved this time, even the kids."

He looked at her, his eyes a bit haunted. "I'll take no chances, honey, I promise. I won't be at work all day. I want to check out this Correy guy, check his widow. I want to see if this was a real person, find out what kind of man he was when he was alive. Also, I think I saw something about an Emby in the *Guardian* recently. Easy to confirm, and I will. Meanwhile, see if you can find our copy."

He opened the door. She had gotten up and moved to the door with him, the fear still plain in her eyes.

"Later, hon," he said, his mind already preoccupied with his plans for the day.

She closed the door behind him.

I spent my waiting time talking to Malcolm and Roy. There was nothing else to do, and I did not feel like just staring at the walls.

When Jim Bronson returned home that evening, Lindsey had settled down a lot. She had her jitters and shakes to a normal level, and she was coping. He told her he would have updated visas by the end of the week.

He had also visited Jadine. I became more attentive.

"She told me he was a good husband and a good father," he said, "but was caught up with Obeah."

They moved to the kitchen and sat down at the table. The children were watching a movie in the front room. Lindsey waited.

"I talked with this Jadine for some time," he said. "She said Obeah killed a good friend recently, Charles Emby, and her husband had tried to get his friend to do something just before it happened and did not succeed."

"Sounds unreal," Lindsey said.

"I think it's real enough," Jim said. "Did you find the *Guardian* for the night this Emby character got himself killed? It's probably in that pile under the coffee table, unless you tossed them in the garbage."

She made no answer.

"Must not have," he continued, "or you would be a little more upset at what I've been saying. It's rough stuff."

He got up, went in the front room and found the paper, then brought it back in the kitchen. He sat again and handed her the *Guardian*. "Here it is," he said. "Take a look. Not nice at all. They really did a number on the guy, and his girlfriend."

Lindsey was already staring at the newspaper, at the front page pictures, speed-reading the story. Her hands shook a little, making it hard for her to continue. Finally, she pushed the paper to one side.

"God," she moaned. "This can't be happening."

Good, I thought. This is going in the right direction.

Tony raced into the room, with Cindy right behind him. "Where's Jessi?" asked Tony. "We can't find her anywhere in the house."

"She's gone," snapped Lindsey in a no-nonsense voice. "She won't be back. She told you goodbye this morning, so drop it and go watch TV."

Not at all satisfied, but cowed by the threat in Lindsey's voice, they ran back to the front room.

"Can we watch a movie on video?" Tony called back.

"The *Star Wars* movie!" chimed Cindy.

"After supper," said Lindsey. "It's ready now."

Later, after supper, Tony impatiently pushed back his chair. "The movie," he said. "You guys promised."

Jim grunted an affirmative and went to place the tape in the machine. I guess he figured it would at least get the kids out of their hair. He rejoined Lindsey in the kitchen, where she was cleaning up after the meal.

I left them, went outside the house, and walked moodily in the front yard among the various flowers and small trees proliferating there.

"Look like you maybe right this time," said Roy, who was sitting near a small banana tree with Malcolm.

"Yeah," I said. "I still don't like it though, forcing them this way."

Roy shrugged, got to his feet. "You get used to it. Fun after while. Me, I used to worry a lot, too."

He shook his head. "No, man, I fight at first. That why Mr. Singh he let Fido work on me plenty. Me, I learn quick. No fun at first, but if survive mean have fun, then I have fun. Don' make no never mind if fun or not fun, I go with the big boy. Now it fun. Done a lot since early, long-time days."

"I don't think I can adjust so quickly," I answered, finally.

"Let we go in dreams tonight?" asked Malcolm. "You going too slow, man. Mr. Singh, he don' like it when we go slow and thing. Let we help man, speed things up."

"Not tonight," I said carefully. "Maybe later."

I thought hard on what Malcolm had said. Was something going on here I didn't know? Was Singh pulling a fast one? "Don' get vex with we when we want to help," Roy said soothingly. "Boring for we, you know. You got something to do. We sit with nothing, waiting for you to drop crumb and thing. Mr. Singh he usually make sure we stay busy and thing."

There it was again, that veiled threat, that hint of how these jobs usually worked.

I relented, a little. "Go tease the neighborhood dogs. Start some confusion there."

"Better than nothing," said Roy.

"Should have let Jessi girl stay a little," Malcolm said. "She fun, that Jessi girl."

"I needed her gone," I told him. "I wanted them to be cut off from anybody native who might give them some hope. Also, I wanted you guys to have some fun."

"Smart move, getting rid of she," Malcolm said. I didn't think he meant it.

"Still wish we had second go at she." Malcolm laughed, watching my face. "No worry, Clark, man. Mr. Singh he say your show, so we wait. If job go bad we take over. Mr. Singh he going be impatient, real quick. Some times he stir things up, you bet. No worry, now, maybe plenty worry later." He grinned.

"Did you pass on my message to Charlie?" I asked, trying to change the subject. "You were going to get word to him through the Marion Fields spirit. I saw Marion at the cemetery, but she wouldn't talk to me. Did you get through?"

"Give she the message," said Roy. "Don' know why she no talk to you, man. Maybe she 'fraid you get her in trouble with all you talk on kill Mr. Singh and thing."

"You told her that?" I asked.

"Sure," he said. "You don' say not tell she. Anyhow, she going try find Charlie for you. If he can get heself together enough, Marion will get he to you for big reunion and thing. I told she we working this place. Maybe she bring he here. Big get together and them. You can all talk 'bout how you want to kill Singh and thing."

"You going to humbug the children, man?" asked Malcolm.

He was not about to accept the change in subject. He wanted something to do.

"No," I growled. "Leave them alone."

Malcolm gave me a disgusted look but said nothing.

We were quiet for a while, then they went to stir up trouble in the neighborhood.

Later that night, I got into Jim's very first dream. No waiting at all.

This time, he was just sitting on his couch in his dream world, playing games with his children. I suggested gently that they leave the room, so big people could talk. Jim looked up at me, and the children disappeared. Not my doing.

He's learning, I thought. That took real control.

"Back again?" he asked. "Thought I had a week or two."

"I just wanted to follow up to be sure you were heading in the right direction." I sat in the arm chair, facing him.

"If you were here all evening, you already know that answer," he said.

Slippery asshole, I thought. Does he think this is some kind of game?

"Jim," I said, "maybe there is a way out of this, but I haven't seen it. Obeah is bad in this country, and you have to do whatever this Singh asks. I'm not sure if it would ever be possible for you to fight him."

"Your wife said you were a good man," Jim said. He was no longer relaxed. He was intent now, trying to make his point. "She was wrong."

"Maybe," I answered. "To my way of thinking, I'm trying to save your ass. I have no choice about being here, but, since I am, I must get you to leave. Fortunately, for you, I was allowed the option of trying persuasion first. From what I've seen your death could well be what happens next if persuasion doesn't work. Do you want to take that chance, Jim?"

"How do I know this danger is real?" he asked.

I glared at him, got up, paced a little. This fool just couldn't seem to get the point. It was his ass in a sling, and he didn't want to believe it.

"Go reread that *Guardian* article," I answered. "Get in touch with Jessi and ask her and her family a few questions. Talk to my wife again. Whatever. I can't do it for you. You have everything you need in the way of proof, and then some."

"I would have to break my contract," he said. "I could get black-balled, we could lose our savings." He was still playing the "reasonable" role.

"You'd still be alive," I snapped, trying to break past that smugness. Being civilized was not going to help him now. "What good is your stupid career if you're dead?" I asked. "See how much good my career is doing me? Or Charlie's career?"

"What if I arrange a leave of absence?" he asked. "Leave a way open to come back later."

By this time I was getting pissed. "I don't give a big rat's ass how you do it," I said, through clenched teeth. "Just get the hell out of this country."

Suddenly he stood, decision stamped all over his face. "I'll get our tax visas," he said. "I'll pick up our plane tickets, contact relatives in the States, and, in general, set things in motion to leave the country. Then I'll make the final decision next week."

"Monday," I countered. "No later than Monday."

"Agreed," he said and woke himself up.

That I did not like. It told me he had learned a lot. Maybe too much.

CHAPTER NINETEEN

I was not happy about waiting until Monday. Supposedly, they had until the Monday after that, but I wasn't willing to wait that long for a decision. I knew from experience you could not get out of this country immediately on deciding to leave.

Malcolm and Roy were furious. They, undoubtedly, had checked with Singh. He must have agreed with me, though, because they did nothing during the waiting period except minor haunting; like flickering lights, pestering the dog, and blaring the television in the night. Silly shit.

I let them do it. I thought it would help keep the pressure on the Bronsons, plus keep my two companions half satisfied. Any extra pressure was welcome.

Even when it got a bit more serious, I said nothing. What the hell, I thought. So Jim gets tripped once or twice, so Lindsey gets her tits massaged. Maybe it will help.

Jessi returned on Saturday, scared but determined, armed with a prayer guard from her grandmother. It was good thinking, but her grandmother evidently did not know how to do the guard and had not gone to a professional for help. The guard was useless.

I let my companions horrors her the same night, while she was awake, to prove to her how futile her preparations were. She took it, grimly, so I told them to leave her alone except in her dreams. I would have had to allow serious injuries to get past that determination, and I did not want that. After all, if the decision were right, she could leave and be out of it. I didn't think Jim would be dumb enough to turn me down, but I did not like this waiting.

There was no sign of Charlie. He had plenty of time to have gotten the message and come here, even if Marion wouldn't. I wondered if he were blaming me for his death and didn't want anything to do with me now.

On Monday, I let Malcolm and Roy know I wanted no humbugging at all. I wanted the household to sleep that night. I knew Jim had the tax visas and airline tickets. He made sure they were visible. He had also made arrangements for movers, but he had told them to wait for his final go-ahead later in the week.

At last, he slept.

His first dream was a nightmare. Snow again. He evidently had a thing about snow. This time his family was with him as he fought his way through a blizzard, on foot.

I banished the snow, sent Lindsey and the children scurrying to a nearby house. I brought out the sun and let Jim see me. We now stood in sunshine in a group of trees, but he still fought to shake off his shivers.

"Pretty good with these dreams," he commented.

"I didn't give you the nightmare," I told him. "Have you made a decision?" I wanted no part of waiting for my answer. I had waited long enough.

"Yeah," he answered. "I'm going to leave on Thursday. I managed to line up a new job, and they're paying my moving expenses."

I grinned, the relief almost palpable. I reached out and shook his hand. "Good," I said. "You made the right decision."

"Maybe so," he answered. "I'm still not happy about it, but I had no choice. For the record, I tried to get an Obeah man or pundit involved, but you were right. I saw three 'supposed' witch doctors, and none of them wanted any part of it."

I gave him a half grin. "I wish I could get out of this that easily," I said, "but I'm stuck with it. Believe me, you are lucky. Don't ever come back."

He appeared a little irritated by my high, good humor. I couldn't blame him, but I could not hide my elation, either. Charlie had been a disaster, but this would help. This one was working right.

The dream wavered, startling both of us.

A small voice screamed from a distance, from outside the dream, and everything shifted once more, like a minor earthquake.

"What the hell?" I growled.

"It's Tony," said Jim. "Must be having a nightmare. I have to wake up and take care of it."

The dream stripped away, and I stepped out.

Tony was screaming at the top volume his lungs could produce, and that top volume was truly awesome. I don't believe I have ever heard that magnitude of sound from so small a source. I could also hear

Cindy, but barely. She was not holding back; she just didn't have the same caliber of lung power.

Jim and Lindsey were both awake, racing for the children's bedroom. They were joined by Jessi as they threw open the kids' bedroom door.

It was bedlam!

Both children were running about, screaming. Malcolm and Roy were there, flinging windows open and shut, shifting furniture, tripping the children, pulling their hair, pinching them, biting them. They twisted arms and pulled ears. They ripped open pillows and strewed shredded foam into the air stream from the fan.

No one but me could see them.

I stared, shocked into immobility. This I had not expected.

"I told you we were leaving!" Jim shouted as he plowed through the debris to the children.

Lindsey and Jessi stood at the door briefly. Then Lindsey joined Jim.

Jessi stayed at the door, making a noise somewhere between a whimper and a strangled scream. She knew what was happening, and she knew everything was out of control. This was major Obeah, and she was out of her depth.

Grinning, Malcolm left the blitzed room, grabbed Jessi by the hair, dragged her, and shoved her into the bedroom and against Lindsey. Both tumbled to the floor in a disorganized heap of panic.

"Stop it!" I yelled, still thinking this was some kind of over-reaction on their part. "I told you shitheads no humbugging! No haunting! They're leaving on Thursday. You're going to screw everything up."

Malcolm gave me a half grin, still excited like hell, but he stopped. Roy joined him, and both stood facing me with uncertain looks on their faces. It was obvious that the uncertainty was only concerned with my reaction. They were not sorry about what they had done.

My blood chilled. This was serious. To disobey me is no big deal, but they would never dare ignore Singh's directions. Singh must have changed their orders. They were proud of being good, team partners, but that would not stop them from acting on new orders.

"We been waiting on you," said Roy. "Hold off til you get here. Only fair. You and we suppose to be team. Not your fault Mr. Singh change things around."

I had it right then. Super trouble.

"Mr. Singh, he cut back the time," added Malcolm, confirming my fears. "He say you too soft. He wants some punish before they go. You letting they slide free. He say he change mind, now he wants this guy dead, and everybody else that get in the way and thing. He send word to we while you still in dream. We figure big scene get you here quick."

"He say you got to help we," said Roy. "Guess he wants you to handle things more different. Big test and thing?"

I looked at them in disbelief. "They've got their plane tickets," I said. "They can get an earlier date. So ease up. Soft or not, I got Singh what he wants."

Roy laughed softly. "You don' understand," he said. "It too late for sure. Mr. Singh say he think about it and thing, and Bronson going to get off too easy. So he don' give we no choice. He tell we to kill someone and make you help. Sorry man, you on team and thing, but Mr. Singh, sometimes he change rules and them, and we have to go with new rules. What we think is no never mind."

"They still have today," I snarled, trying to think of a way out, knowing it was hopeless.

"No, man," said Roy. "Too late. No more deadline. He no care about Bronson leaving and thing. He want he dead and that be our new job. Maybe white man do something else to get Mr. Singh so vex. Whatever, it way too late now."

"I won't let you," I snapped.

"Better not try that again," advised Malcolm. "Remember last time? You don' hurt we, and Emby fellow die anyhow. Besides, this still your job. Rules changed, but you still part of team."

We were all in the front room by then. Jim was on the phone, arguing with someone at the airport. It was too late for anyone from any of the airlines to be there, but early enough that someone was there.

"Can't get away until tomorrow," he told Lindsey. His face was white. "We'll go to a hotel, get out of here, get out of this house. Then we'll leave Trinidad tomorrow morning. Best we can manage."

He opened the door.

Malcolm tore it from his grasp, slammed it and locked it, then did something to the lock.

"Let them go!" I exclaimed. "You heard him on the phone and afterwards. They'll leave here now and be gone in the morning. That should satisfy Singh."

"Sorry, man," Roy said. "We like you, man, but we don' fight Mr. Singh. He give we job, and we stuck with it. More better you help we, like you told. No way you can help these people. Still your decision, man."

I heard a muffled scream and turned to see Malcolm stuffing a teddy bear down Jessi's throat, holding her down and stuffing it with the heel of his shoe.

"No!" I blurted.

My rage came to the fore, blocking off rationality. I rushed Malcolm, half gibbering, only to be tripped by Roy. I slid into the wall, stopped.

"Last warning," Roy said. "No interfere. You don' help, we understand. Mr. Singh, he screw you on this. If you don' help, just leave we here but don' fight we."

I threw him to one side, my rage giving me a strength I did not know I had. I scrambled to Jessi, using the video machine as a club to knock Malcolm away, and started prying the teddy bear loose.

I was too late. Jessi was already dead.

This can't be happening, I thought. This can't be happening, not again.

I looked up from Jessi, looked at Roy who was watching me expectantly, looked at the Bronson family who were huddled to one side while Jim frantically tried to get the door open, looked at Malcolm who had gotten back to his feet and was moving toward the Bronsons once more. I looked at Roy, trying to get my rage under control, trying to think straight.

"Better leave we," said Roy. "You already in deep shit. Fido and Birdbrain already on way. Better you stop now 'cause the big boys be here soon."

Malcolm stopped, watching me, waiting to see what my response might be.

Birdbrain? I wondered. That has to be one of the bird things, those vulture looking things.

"This our job now, man," said Malcolm. "Mr. Singh he say stop they clock. Don' mind cover for you, but we going to finish job."

Malcolm turned from me and moved back toward Lindsey. I felt something snap in my mind, my priorities stumbled into place, and I knew I was committed.

I seized a large umbrella, spun Malcolm around, and thrust the umbrella at him as if it were a sword. He had been busy ripping off Lindsey's clothes, and he turned on me, enraged at my decision, my interference.

I rammed the umbrella point into and through his eye. He screamed and fell to one side. I broke off the umbrella, leaving the tip end in his eye, then decided what was left was too flimsy. I looked around the room, glanced out the door, saw a hammer Jim had left laying in the hallway. I stepped out, and picked it up for an attack on Roy.

Whatever I need, I thought, already comfortable with my decision and determined.

Malcolm and Roy moved off to one side, glaring at me. The umbrella point had been removed. The eye was healed as if nothing had happened. I watched them, warily, knowing they had not given up, not these two. They were deciding how to handle me.

They watched me. They watched the hammer. What are these two waiting for? Then I remembered. Reinforcements on the way.

Suddenly, Malcolm was up and running across the floor. He had the umbrella point in one hand, and he was using it like a dagger, straight at Cindy's open mouth.

I hit Cindy from the side, and knocked her out of the way. I pulled her out of the room and out the back door. I locked the door so she couldn't get back in.

Please, I thought. Run to a neighbor's house.

I found they were now in the dining room with me, Malcolm and Roy still harrassing the Bronsons. I brushed Roy to one side and went for Malcolm with the hammer.

Jim had Lindsey and Tony with him, all of them now gathered at the back door, trying to get out to join Cindy. While I pounded Malcolm with the hammer, Roy slammed the back door and trapped Lindsey inside. Jim and Tony were out of the house. I could hear him moving the kids away.

He'll be back in here, I thought. For Lindsey. I returned my full attention to Malcolm, to Roy, wondering what the hell else I could do.

"Come on, Clark, give up," came Charlie's voice. "You can't stop them, no more than you could save me. It's time to leave."

"She's still alive," I screamed. "You have to help me."

I couldn't see him. No matter. He was here.

"Shit," came Charlie's answer. "I can't even help myself. I haven't figured out how to do much more than talk and walk. Marion brought me here, couldn't stay. She didn't know this was going on."

"She knew," I growled. "She don't want to help, and you can't."

"Get your ass out of here," he insisted.

"Get the hell out of my way," I snarled.

He did. I saw him moving, almost like a shadow. Then he was gone, outside I guessed. I could also hear Jim and the kids outside, not far. I knew Jim was trying to get back in for Lindsey.

Malcolm and Roy had been watching, waiting to see if Charlie would get me out of their hair. Seeing Charlie leave, Malcolm came at me, and Roy moved to Lindsey.

I took Malcolm out with the hammer, and moved for Roy. He had a kitchen knife, and stabbed Lindsey in the side even as I hit him with the hammer. I got the door open, and shoved her out. I turned back to the fray.

I heard Jim cry out, and heard noises that told me he was getting her and the kids to the car. Lindsey had been injured seriously, but she was alive.

Just get to a neighbor's house, I thought. Singh won't escalate to another family.

The car started. I tried to keep Malcolm and Roy in the house, but no luck.

We all boiled out the door together. The car was moving with Jim and his family inside. I prepared for fresh battle, but they had stopped in the yard, watching.

Jim rammed the accelerator too hard and crashed into two parked cars across the road. Something huge swooped from the sky, then, just as Jim helped Lindsey and the kids out of the car and started them moving for the nearest house with lights showing. The vulture thing landed on Jim's shoulders and lifted him in the air. Lindsey hobbled down the street, urging the children to move faster.

Jim pulled free, falling almost ten feet to the ground. He followed his family. Nothing followed.

Singh's crew must have territorial limitations, I thought. Or this is enough to satisfy Singh. At least the Bronsons appear to be out of it. Now how about me?

"That's it," said Charlie. "Now we get lost."

I looked at him. Still not much more than an outline, but at least I could see him.

"Come on," Charlie insisted. "Those people seem safe enough, so now we make tracks before the whole crew comes after us."

"Charlie, I've got to get to Jadine. Singh will kill her."

Then we were both running. Charlie seemed more visible every moment.

Fido appeared, huge and frightening, blocking our escape. He had me even as I tried to slip to one side. He shook me, hard, a preliminary gesture.

I guess he was too eager. He shook too hard, and I fell free. Charlie dragged me to my feet, and we were away and moving fast before the thing even realized I was free.

We rushed through a nearby gate, then crashed into underbrush beyond the house. Fido followed for a while, then I did not hear him. I saw Birdbrain's shadow once, but we flattened ourselves, and he passed over.

For some reason, neither Malcolm nor Roy joined the search. Maybe lack of instructions, possibly they wanted me to escape to see how Singh would react, who knows.

CHAPTER TWENTY

I stumbled, cursed and moved across town, heading for home, for Jadine and my children. My fear was almost a living thing, my fear for my family.

Charlie was with me, and it helped. Just knowing I was not alone was a fantastic gift. I guess he knew how I felt, for he said nothing. He stayed with me.

I reached the house and could not enter. Belatedly, I remembered the guard I told Jadine to get. I now saw it as a mistake.

I was afraid I would have to wait for night, hoping and praying Singh did not see Malcolm and Roy before I could reach Jadine and warn her off.

I turned to Charlie. "Any ideas?"

"Hell, you've been dead longer than me," he answered. "You seem to be doing pretty good now."

"Where did Marion find you?" I asked. I kept trying doors and windows, attempting to gain entry. Finally, I stopped, turned to Charlie. "Well," I asked. "Where did she find you, and how did you find me?"

"I was still at my house," he answered. "She told me somebody called Roy told her where to find you. Told her you might be a little busy. She brought me here and took off." Charlie's face mirrored his unhappiness and uncertainty. "She was a lot friendlier before she died," he complained.

"Yeah," I answered absently. "She's had a lot happen to her since then."

Frustrated, I continued to prowl around the house until Jadine emerged, ready to go to work, just as a babysitter arrived.

I moved toward her and was stopped. She had the guard. I could not touch her, and I could not enter the house after she was gone.

"I've got to follow her," I told Charlie. "I have to know she isn't hit by Singh before I can talk to her."

"Go on," he said. "I'll stay here and make sure no one sets a trap while you're gone."

"Great." I moved away, following Jadine.

I followed her across town to her work. She was cashier at JP Supermarket in St. James. I hoped she would forget and remove the guard, but it did not happen. I followed her home again that evening, and, once more, was forced to wait outside.

Charlie let me know there had been no visitors. At precisely seven, I found I could enter the house. Charlie stayed outside, so nothing would surprise me. Frantically, I flickered the lights.

Startled, she reached for her guard, then stopped, her eyes questioning.

"Clark? Is that you?"

I hit the lights.

"You need to talk to me?"

Again, the lights.

She stood, went to the bathroom, and took a bottle of sleeping tablets from the medicine cabinet.

No, I thought. Those will keep you out too long.

She swallowed the medicine, two or three capsules, made sure the children were tucked in, and lay down on the couch to relax.

The medicine worked. I just hoped she hadn't taken too much. She was not going to be able to stay asleep. She would have to get herself awake as soon as I finished talking to her.

She slept, and I entered the first dream.

She was on our beach, nude. My agitation affected the dream world so that storm clouds formed and the sea turned angry. Jadine sat up and looked at me; a bathing suit appeared.

Quickly, I told her what happened and what I feared might happen. I saw her face change from incredulity to horror and finally to fear.

"The children!" she cried.

"Not yet," I said soothingly, calmer since my story was out. "We're probably safe enough for now, and you have a good guard. Besides, they can't move without Singh's instructions, and they can't get those before later tonight at the earliest. More likely, we have a few days, but I suppose we have to assume Singh will get his crew organized tonight, that tomorrow night is too late."

She watched me, waiting.

"When you wake up," I continued, "you have to book a flight out, any flight, anywhere, just so it's out of here. If you can get it tonight, take it. If it has to be morning then head for the airport first thing. If you're awake enough it might not be a bad idea to go to the Bel Air tonight."

"The sleeping pills," she said, groaning.

"Yeah. That might keep you out for hours, but maybe I can help get you awake faster. At least long enough to make the flight reservations. Then play it by ear. If you're awake enough to drive to the Bel Air, do it. Otherwise leave first thing in the morning."

She clung to me. "You away from him. Stay away. He destroy you."

I laughed, a bitter laugh with no humor to it. "Huh-uh, baby. He can always find me, so I might as well go to him and get it over with. That way, maybe I can buy time for you and the kids. It's too late for me. Maybe Charlie can help, if I can figure out how to use him."

"Elizabeth call me," she said. "They going to move your body. Soon."

"Great," I answered. I stared off at the ocean landscape. "Now I have a chance to get free, but you have to get out of the country. I have to know you and the kids are safe. It's time to get you awake."

She sat up, made patterns in the sand with her toes.

"No," she said. "I still all sleepy and shaky from the pill if you wake me now. It too soon. I have to think clear when I start making calls and thing. Besides, I have things you need to know. Very important."

"Can't be helped," I said.

"Clark, I have he name."

I was rising to my feet, but I froze on that.

"What?" It had to sink in. I had not expected this. "Singh's name?" I asked, incredulous. "What is it? You really know?"

"Yes," she replied. "He name is Baal Ramish. You have to say it three times. He live on Tragarete Road, number seventy-two."

"How'd you find out?" I asked.

"Didn't," she said. "It was Charles had the idea. He don' like Singh, and he find that not he real name. He check through government records and birth certificates until he find reference and thing to true name. He find where real name kept."

She snuggled closer to me, knowing this was what I needed and knowing I would leave soon, that I would try to use this.

"He send all he notes and thing to me," she said. "I got letter after he die, and Krishna check he notes and he get name and address for me. I wait for you to come back, to tell you."

So now I had it all, maybe. If the body move was in time. If I could figure out how to use the name.

We made small talk then, to allow time for the sleeping pill to wear down. We made love; rough, frantic, clutching, but not too satisfying. Slowly, we relaxed a little.

Finally, I got up, conscious our time was over. I hoped we hadn't cut it too fine. "Listen," I said. "It's time, time for you to wake up. You have to call the airlines."

She cried, but she agreed. Shortly afterwards, she was awake, with the help of a glass of ice water. I waited to hear her make reservations with BWIA for a morning flight to Miami. She looked groggy as hell, so I knew she'd have to spend the night here, get a little sleep.

Can't be helped, I thought. I left the house. Charlie joined me as I came out the side door.

There was only one place to go, and that was Singh's house. We reached there shortly after midnight. He was not home, and I could not enter. I even tried using the name, the old "open sesame" syndrome, but nothing happened.

This I had expected. No surprises.

I saw no signs of other precautions. He had taken such care to hide his name that he did not appear to be overly concerned with security here.

I asked Charlie to go back and stay with Jadine. At least she wouldn't be alone. I gave him the name, also. I had no false hopes about his ability to help, but at least he would have as much as I had.

I settled outside Singh's house to wait, sitting in a mango tree, feeling hopeful. His pets would not look for me here. He would not dare have them here, where access to his real life would be open to them. Might not matter, I thought. He will keep it from the spirits, but it won't make any difference to the things like Fido. They want him alive.

I wondered where Singh was, why he was so late. Then, with a flash of horror, I realized that he must be at his meeting place, possibly with Malcolm and Roy.

It looked as if time had already run out.

I almost left then. I almost went back to Jadine. Then I remembered Charlie and the Bronsons, how much help I had been. If I were going to help, it had to be here. I had to apply the name weapon, and I had to be where Malcolm and Roy wouldn't find me. Maybe I'd get lucky and the Obeah things wouldn't come with Singh when he finally came home.

I waited.

CHAPTER TWENTY ONE

The waiting was terrible. My mind kept presenting scenarios for me to contemplate, visions of Singh chaining me beneath the ocean, of Fido joyously ripping at me, of Malcolm and Roy tackling Jadine and our children. Worse yet, I suffered through graphic images of Charlie dying, of Jessi and the teddy bear.

Baal Ramish, Jadine had said. The name on the mailbox confirmed only that P. Singh lived here. It seemed he had buried his real name so deep he didn't even use it for his mail. This whole venture could be an exercise in futility. Someone so strong in Obeah surely would not be careless enough to depend entirely on this name thing. There has to be something; either the name is worthless as a weapon, or he has something else to protect him.

I could detect nothing, and I had no other options left in any event.

I nursed my rage, I nursed my grief. I held to my emotions, trying to draw all the strength I could.

I waited.

Finally, I saw lights coming up the deserted street and the turn signal activated for the driveway. Singh was coming home, alone. I saw no sign of his wife and had to assume she was in the house, probably asleep, which meant Singh had been on business his wife was not concerned with.

My rage took hold once more, driving out the fear. I gripped that rage like a weapon and waited for Singh near the door.

He parked in the garage, carefully locked his car, and moved to the house. I saw no sign of Fido, no shadows to warn of horrors from the sky. He was alone, apparently unconcerned, safe in his clothing of anonymity.

I moved very close, dogging his footsteps, almost merging with him.

When he opened the door and entered his house, I was with him. I was past his house guard. I grinned tightly, following him to his bedroom.

With great difficulty, I managed to keep from tackling him immediately. I could have. I almost did. I resisted that urge for an immediate attack, and impatiently waited in that bedroom.

I wanted him to know who he was dealing with. I wanted him to feel fear in his heart. I wanted him to beg for mercy, and I wanted him dead, but not too quickly.

He has to pay, I thought. Before he dies he has to pay.

There were no more thoughts of failure, there was no more fear of Singh.

He was alone in the house, except for his wife, and I was sure that even if he allowed his pets within the house he would not have them in his bedroom. So I felt a little more secure as we moved into that bedroom.

I waited while he made himself comfortable next to his wife, while he went to sleep. He did not seem to be concerned about anything, not in the slightest. He had no fears to keep him awake, no uncertainties to hold back slumber.

He slept.

I entered his first dream.

It was a very ordinary everyday dream setting, somewhere in West Moorings near the ocean. I saw a solitary fisherman and knew it had to be Singh. I walked toward him, taking no precautions. I knew I was safe there within the dream.

As I neared, I saw he was not fishing. He was tormenting spirits he had chained beneath the waves. I was not sure how I knew that, because his actions were ambiguous, but I knew. I was also aware it was a real torture session, that those lost souls felt his ministrations even though he was dreaming, and far from West Moorings.

I say *chained*, but these were not like any chains I had ever seen in real life. I called them chains because that was the word I had heard used for what I was seeing.

The spirits beneath the water bore little resemblance to the mortals they once had been. They had been allowed to rot, they had been nibbled at, they had been ignored and, then, tormented. The chains were not chains, rather they appeared to be gossamer thin tatters of filth. They held the spirits captive and apparently caused agonizing pain whenever they touched a spirit body. It was monstrous!

He saw me and straightened from whatever he was doing and turned to face me, not frightened at all. I had expected some fear, for now he knew I was aware of where he lived. The name I would not reveal until I was ready to use it, and that would not be until crunch time.

"Ah, Mr. Correy, how did you learn my whereabouts?"

I saw no reason to hide it. It was much too late for that and could make no difference.

"Charlie dug it out," I said, "a little before you killed him."

"Yes, I see how it must have happened quite clearly," he said, amiably. "I should have disposed of Mr. Emby earlier, but I wanted him to make me some money first. I did not believe he knew the importance of a name to Obeah, and I may have been a little careless. Oh well, what's done is done. What can I do for you?"

His matter-of-fact attitude ground into my rage, sharpening it to a fine point. I felt my body stiffen. My fists clenched. "I've come to kill you, and I wanted you to know it was me."

He smiled. "Really now, Mr. Correy, I am sure you must be aware you cannot kill in the dream world. Tell me, do you wish me to wake at once, or do you wish to talk further?"

"I have nothing more to say," I growled. I was a little worried. He was too calm, too sure of himself. I smelled a trap.

"Ah, but I do," he said, confirming my fears. "I would like you to see what is in store for you."

Suddenly I was in the water with him, staring in horror at the half-real remnant of a man there. Fish nibbled at him, and his mouth was open in a perpetual scream. Chains of filth held him in place. Waves battered him. He was unable to escape, embroiled in a torture far worse than any living creature ever had to endure.

And that man was Charlie!

My mind shied from the implications. It skittered out of control for a moment then returned.

Was it already too late for Jadine?

With all my strength, I pulled us back to the shore, shaken. I then realized I succeeded only because he allowed it. Always before, I had complete control over the dream world. Singh was in control here.

This was an aspect of Obeah I had not expected, and Singh had me completely off balance. Which is what he wants. This man is formidable, with strength even in his dream. What the hell do I do now? I wondered.

I tried to change the topography of the dream, to get control back. Nothing.

"Ah, you are surprised," he said, delighted. "Do you wish a preliminary bout here, or will you tackle me in the real world?"

I just glared, my mind in turmoil.

"Come, come," he continued. "I am sure you recognized Mr. Emby. One of my pets found him earlier where he had no business. I have no need for additional staff at the moment, so I have added him to my little underwater collection. You will join him shortly."

He had said nothing about Jadine, so he had done nothing, yet. He would have said something, could not have resisted gloating. The only thing that had changed was that Charlie had gotten caught. If I could kill Singh, that, too, would end.

"You wish a test of strength?" he asked again, enjoying himself.

"You're bluffing," I said. "Maybe you've learned some control of your own dreams, but that won't help you when you wake up."

His grin broadened. He did something with one hand, and the thing that had been Charlie gave a soundless scream that echoed through my head.

He continued to grin. "With all that confidence," he said, "I have to assume you learned my name as well as my address. Very resourceful, I must say. Now you have the idea it will help you. You are so naive. It's really a pity. You would have been a strong addition to my staff. I appreciate strength. Too bad I have to terminate our relationship."

"It's you that will die," I said. "Tell me, out of curiosity. Did you order the Bronsons killed so I could be tested?"

"Not exactly," he replied. "You had succeeded in your persuasions, so I ordered the family spared. However, I instructed your former companions to make it look as though death for all was my object. So, yes, a test of your reactions was involved. It was only a little different from your thoughts."

Great, I thought. So my rebellion had been for nothing. But how could I have known that?

"Tell me something, now," he continued. "How did you plan to kill me? I shall no doubt find your proposed methods informative. I may even allow you a few extra hours of freedom if your inventiveness amuses me."

He is the most egotistical bastard I have ever known, I thought. I glared at him and did not answer his question. Why should I tell him I had no idea how I would kill him, that I was just winging it, playing it by ear?

"Mr. Correy," he now said, "I do not intend to wait for an answer. It does not hold my interest at the moment. However, I am quite pleased to discover your endeavors to learn my name. Knowing who discovered my name will make it possible for me to ensure this never happens again."

I grimaced. I would have to watch my mouth. This bastard doesn't miss a trick.

"Mr. Correy," he said, "I now have everything I need from you, and I have shown you what I wished to show you. I believe you can now be dispensed with, and we shall end this farce of a conversation."

My brain flashed an alert.

Get out of here! was the message. This is a trap!

I ignored it.

"Bluffing again," I growled. "Go ahead and wake up. I would just as soon finish our business, also."

I tried to pull free from the dream, to finish him before he woke up. I could not.

Something about the dream held me in place. Earlier, I had not been able to change the dream, now I could not leave it.

I looked at him. He gazed back, amused. So he is holding me. There's no doubt of it. Somehow he has pinned me here.

He laughed that special laugh again. "Please, note," he said, waving his hand to indicate my predicament, "you cannot leave until I wake up. Then we merge together, briefly. I do not have to hold you long. You must admit this gives our game a little zip. I would not wish for you to think you had an unfair advantage over me. It might upset your conscience."

He laughed, a little louder. "You should have killed me when you first entered the house. You could have succeeded then quite easily.

You are not only boring, you are also an idiot. You could have won!"

He's telling the truth, I thought. I had my shot and sloughed it off.

"You can't keep holding me," I said.

"No," he answered, " only until I wake up, which will be very soon now. First, I want you to know what's happening. It is always amusing if the victim knows in advance what will happen."

"Nothing is happening," I snapped. "You're stalling. Okay, so you can hold me for a while, but sooner or later you'll wake up, and then your ass is mine."

"Such persistence," he said. "Listen, Mr. Correy, listen to me. When you entered my bedroom, you saw my wife. She is quite adept in Obeah herself, as I believe you know. Roy or Malcolm will have told you, I'm sure. While talking to you, I also was in contact with her through the dream medium. She has already contacted one of my pets, the one you call Birdbrain. You won't really have time to do anything, I'm afraid."

"You're bluff—"

Singh awoke.

The sound of wings filled the room, and a terrible stench. I was held, seemingly within Singh, for a fraction of time. Then I was thrust to one side. Singh rolled quickly from the bed. I made an abortive grab for him, but claws already dipped into my flesh and pulled me loose before I could consolidate my grip. Singh was free.

I struggled, trying to break clear. The thing was just holding me; no ripping, no tearing. I kept trying to escape, but to no avail. The bird thing had only one thought, if it thought at all, and that was to be sure I was held in place pending Singh's orders on where I was to be taken.

As I waited, while Singh got dressed, I raged at myself for my selfishness in wanting Singh to know it was me, for not killing him at once, for not even trying to use the name weapon, for not understanding his confidence had to have some basis, for grossly underestimating my enemy. I had lost, completely lost, and with the element of surprise gone there was no chance left.

No chance here, I thought, but Jadine still might escape, and my exhumation is still scheduled. Singh might yet forestall either of these things, but, at least, I can hope he doesn't know; and if he doesn't know then some of his plans will fail.

"Mr. Correy," he said. "I can no longer see you, but I know you are there. Please hear me. My little pet will now take you to West Moorings. You remember the scene in the dream, I'm sure. I will follow in my car and set up the proper Obeah lights so I can observe you as I take care of your incarceration."

He turned his back, and the vulture thing dragged me screaming through the window and flew away, impaling me on one huge talon as soon as we were clear of the house.

It was a short flight. Birdbrain dropped me near the very location I remembered from Singh's dream then stood guard to be sure I waited, which I did after my first few attempts at escape failed miserably.

It was complete overkill. If I had underestimated Singh, it looked as if he had overestimated me. I could see no chances of attack or escape, and my one, good opportunity had slipped from my grasp. Now I was about to pay the price, and maybe Jadine as well.

All too soon, I spotted the lights of Singh's car as he parked near the approach to the sea wall, then watched his flashlight bobbing as he hurried toward where I waited with my winged attendant. He carried a small, canvas bag in one hand, which obviously contained his Obeah equipment. His other hand held a small cage containing a black rooster. Quickly he finished his preparations and lit his flares. The rapidly shifting patterns of light gave an eerie cast to the scene.

Wonder what the locals think of this, I thought.

Then I found myself staring at the rooster's glazed eyes. He had placed the head facing me, and I seemed to be rooted to my present position, held by those dead eyes.

I could not move.

Singh did his usual trance thing. I remained fixed in place. Then Singh looked at me and the spell was broken, if spell it had been. I stared back.

"Ah, this is better. I always like to see my staff clearly. Especially when they are about to become ex-staff."

He turned to the bird thing and made a gesture, and it took to the air.

Immediately, I jumped for Singh but recoiled as if I hit a brick wall. I could not reach him at all. I tried to move away and found I could not do that, either.

It was those damn rooster eyes. They still had me pinned, somehow. Singh chuckled. "Sorry, but you will have to wait, my friend."

"For what?" I snapped.

"I've sent my feathered pet to bring a member of my staff. I always use staff members in these chaining ceremonies. They see what happens, and it keeps them from getting any ideas themselves. I am a great believer in object lessons."

I sat down. Might as well be comfortable, I thought. This guy is long-winded as hell.

I had no inclination to stop the flow of words. There was always the possibility he might let something slip. Despite everything, I had not yet given up. I refocused my attention. I didn't want to miss anything.

"It's really a pity," he was saying. "It's such a waste to put you below. You have shown real fortitude and imagination. I never had a spirit come so close to harming me. Such persistence could be very useful in my work. Yes, very useful." He studied me. "No, you are much too dangerous. I can't keep you around."

"You can't keep me chained forever," I said.

"Oh, can't I?" He chuckled softly. "Once chained, only an Obeah master can free you. It might happen, once I die. But you, then, would work for him, and you would be very damaged, probably insane."

I said nothing. I was not about to voice my hopes about the exhumation of my body and how it might pull me free from his chains.

I was hoping and praying the whole business with Singh would take long enough for Jadine to get clear. That he would go for her, I never doubted, but, for the time being, he was preoccupied with me.

"I hope you are not planning additional attacks," he said. "I would prefer not to damage you too severely before our little adventure. It makes things so messy when I have to have a spirit scraped and shoveled into the chains."

I stood. "Some day, one of your trusted staff will get past your guards and finish you off."

He laughed. He was in high, good humor. "That is possible," he said. "It's always the danger in Obeah. However, you will not be that one, Mr. Correy. After tonight, I will be done with you, and, please, I want you to remember an earlier promise. When you're whiling away the hours with the fish nibbling at you, I want you to remember your widow. I promised that your fighting me would involve her. I now promise your wife will die, that I will recruit her spirit for my staff."

He watched me, pleased. "One more morsel," he continued. "I will make arrangements to adopt your orphaned children. I will be complimented for my compassion. The children will fill the empty gap in my childless life. Of course, I will teach them to be adept in the arts of Obeah. I must pass on my skills."

My blood ran cold. His plans for Jadine and the children were much worse than my wildest imaginings.

I heard the sound of wings as Birdbrain returned, carrying something which he dropped at my feet. It was a woman, or once was. She was naked. Her face and breasts had been fed on by some animal. One foot was missing, but I remembered that had not slowed her, for it was Marion. She bore no resemblance to the Marion I remembered from before her death, but I could remember her from the cemetery. It was her.

"This is Marion Fields, and she is American," Singh said, not noticing I had recognized her.

I cleared my face, to avoid giving that away, too. I returned my attention to Singh.

"She gave me problems at one time," he was saying, "and Fido was a little overzealous. This was in earlier days, before he learned restraint. She is a very good worker, now, never gives me any problems. Still, I think tonight's undertaking might be good for her to see."

He turned from me to Marion, who was staring at him with pure hatred. It was obvious she would kill Singh, herself, if given the opportunity. Malcolm and Roy had been right. She had avoided me earlier because her hatred would not have allowed her to refuse me, and she had been afraid I was not up to the job.

She had been right.

"Marion, meet Mr. Correy, Mr. Clark Correy," said Singh. "He used to work for me, but he decided I should be terminated. Very unwise of Mr. Correy."

He paused. "He happens to be a good friend of the Emby fellow," he continued, "the one we put down here earlier tonight. I'm sure you remember Mr. Emby also, don't you Miss Fields? After all, you helped me forge the chains."

She continued to glare at Singh, but said nothing.

I said, "I thought you would use Roy or Malcolm. After all, they've been with me from the start."

"Ah, Mr. Correy's tongue is working again."

"Not so well as yours," I growled.

"Even insults! I'm very surprised."

He laughed, turned back to Marion. "Please bring Mr. Emby out, Miss Fields. I think Mr. Correy needs to have a better look. The dream vision was perhaps not clear enough."

Obediently, Marion moved to the water's edge, her walk uneven but not a problem to her, either. She stopped, gave Singh another look of pure hatred, and waited.

"Yes," breathed Singh, almost in a whisper. "It is definitely time for you to observe again, my dear Miss Fields. If I were you, I sincerely believe you should proceed with your assigned chores."

Marion advanced into the water, taking her time, and soon was below the surface.

The ocean must shelve off rapidly from this point of West Moorings, I found myself thinking. The fishing boat I had seen earlier was pulling in its anchor. Did her captain or crew feel something, or were they just noticing the Obeah lights?

"Miss Fields was very good-looking once," Singh commented, "and very willful. She still has these little spells where she tries to show her displeasure, not that it does her any good."

The surface of the water broke as Marion emerged, dragging something.

"Please move nearer to the water, Mr. Correy," said Singh, softly.

Damned if I will! I thought, but I found myself moved there.

I tried to break past whatever held me in place and kept me from Singh, but there was no easing on that. Whatever was to come, there was no running. I could not get at Singh, and I could not avoid moving to the shore. My movements were controlled.

Fearfully, I looked down at what Marion had retrieved from the bottom of the ocean. It was Charlie. What was left of him.

The face was eaten away down to the skull on one side, the hand on that side had one finger, and something had taken a large bite out just above one hip. One eye was completely gone, and the remaining eye was locked on me, pleading.

"I may have to lessen the reality spell," murmured Singh. "Mr. Emby appears to be losing his pieces a little too quickly."

The filthy chains lay soggily on the ground, still intact. The stench was terrifying. The thing that had been Charlie couldn't talk, for he no longer had a mouth, but I felt his need to communicate like a very large club hammering at my head.

Startled, I looked at Singh. Nothing. I risked a glance at Marion. She was staring at me, waiting. Charlie was trying to get through, despite his pain and everything that had happened to him. He was trying to tell me something, something important.

I concentrated.

What? I asked, as if to myself. What is it? What are you trying to say? What am I missing? Talk to me. Please, talk to me.

Nothing.

I returned my attention to Singh, who was talking once more. "You mentioned Roy and Malcolm earlier," he said. "I'm sorry, but they are busy tonight. I had a little job for them."

"Humbugging some kids, I suppose," I muttered.

"Not really," he replied. "You see, they saw me earlier tonight, and let me know you had escaped. Of all my staff, you were the only one I ever felt might be capable of finding where my home was located. Which means, of course, that I half expected you there."

I stared at him, cold fingers of comprehension already touching my heart.

"Ah, I see you start to understand." He nodded. "Yes, I sent them to visit your widow. I have uses for her in the very near future, so I am afraid your children will become orphans tonight. In fact, it may already have happened."

My rage was rapidly taking full possession of me, negating the fear that had me immobilized. I found myself moving toward Singh, but he just stood there, unafraid, watching me with a small smile playing across his lips.

I'm doing exactly what he wants, I thought. He's playing me like a puppet of some kind.

I glanced at Charlie, my attention pulled to him despite my confrontation with Singh.

"Use it!"

It was Charlie. It was in my head, and the force of it almost tore my head off.

"Use it!"

I knew what he meant!

I turned my full attention back to Singh, my sudden purposefulness forcing his smile to waver a bit.

"You rotten bastard!" I said. "I know you, you bastard! I know you, Baal Ramish! You are Baal Ramish. Baal Ramish."

Three times, I thought.

He had a sudden look of fear on his face, and I was past his defense.

I did not wait. I rammed my hand into his chest, reached for and found his heart and, using the technique I had learned from Singh himself, I made my hand half-real and started squeezing Singh's heart.

I felt Birdbrain's talons take me and sink in, and I felt him starting to rise. I ignored it, and held on, squeezing and ripping and yelling *Baal Ramish* over and over as Birdbrain lifted both Singh and I into the air.

Then Singh fell into the water, but his heart remained in my hand, still in spasms.

I threw the heart toward the shore, saw it hit at the edge of the water. It was high tide. The heart would lay exposed on the ground as the tide rolled out.

On the shore, I heard Marion laughing wildly, with not even the slightest hint of sanity in her laughter.

Birdbrain faltered.

Then his talons loosened, and both of us fell into the sea.

I knew he was dying. Only Singh's magic had kept him alive. The other monstrocities, too, would die, but not the spirits, not Malcolm, not Roy.

They were with Jadine!

CHAPTER TWENTY TWO

As I hit the water, I remembered Jadine's tales of how a spirit could not take water. I also remembered Singh's plans to chain me within the ocean, and what Charlie had looked like after his stay under water. I panicked!

After all that had happened, all I had accomplished, now, at the last, a simple bath would wipe out everything.

Nothing happened. I found I could move as easily through water as on land. The panic had been stupid. After all, Marion had gone in to drag Charlie out, and all the chained spirits were surviving. However, in a crisis one's brain does not always make sensible choices.

Frantic, I moved for the shore. I ignored Marion, who still was laughing near the rendered-useless Obeah flares. I started running, stumbling along the shoreline toward home.

I left Charlie there, with his still-intact chains. I could do nothing without help from someone. Perhaps Marion could do something for him, if she could get her senses back. Meanwhile I had to think of my family, of Jadine. Charlie was already dead, but Jadine was not.

I pounded along the Diego Martin Main Road, trying to move faster. I was afraid I might be too late. My only real hope was that they would decide to take their time to prolong their fun. Maybe they would horrors her dreams before tackling her in real life. My blood chilled at the thought, but it was Jadine's only chance.

I burst onto the street to my house and slowed to organize my pounding thoughts. I strove to make plans, to decide how to handle things, how to proceed. I knew from bitter experience how difficult my task might be, but I had to succeed. This time it was Jadine.

The guard was in place.

At first, I was relieved. A quick search showed no sign of Malcolm and Roy outside. My fears grew, again. I felt somehow they had gained entry.

I raged outside, checking the windows. From Jadine's bedroom, I heard cries and moans. I looked in. She was asleep, in the throes of a nightmare.

Still time, I thought. Still time, if I can just get in. They're still playing.

Every window was sealed, as were the front and back doors. I was blocked.

I returned to the children's bedroom window and looked in. Jamie and Karen were sleeping peacefully in the same bed, the baby in his crib. In desperation, I pounded on the window then tormented the dog until he howled. I chased him to the window and made him keep howling. I hated that, he was a good dog. However, my need was greater than his comfort.

Jamie woke, came to the window, opened it. "Hush, dog," he said.

I was through, entering in that instant, and, as I did, Malcolm and Roy boiled in behind me. They had not managed entry after all. They pushed past me and moved to Jadine's bedroom. She had not replaced her guard after I left.

I ran after them, only to meet Malcolm, who wielded a club and smashed me into a corner. Jadine was on the bed, screaming. Roy had ripped off her clothes, and she was bleeding badly from a slash on her arm. Her mouth and nose were bleeding also.

I knocked Roy free, wrested the club from Malcolm, and beat Roy to the floor. Waving the club wildly, I had them away from her temporarily.

"How he get past Fido?" asked Malcolm. "Fido down at end of street. Fido should have caught he."

"How he get away from Mr. Singh?" Roy countered.

"Singh's dead," I said, "and so is Fido. You're both free, so leave her alone. You've got no business here now, not with Singh gone."

I circled and tried to get in a better position, watching their every move. As the action slowed, Jadine quickly slipped out of the room. Then I heard her running for the children's room.

"Mr. Singh dead?" Malcolm asked, incredulous. "How he die? You kill he?"

I nodded. Relieved, I saw they had both transferred their attention to me. They weren't chasing Jadine.

"How?" asked Roy. "How he die?"

"I learned his real name and used it, and Fido died when he died.

That's why Fido couldn't stop me."

"Don' believe it," said Malcolm.

"Believe it," I said. "No more Fido. No more Singh. I dug out his heart, and now he's under the ocean at West Moorings. Go see for yourself. Marion is still there, laughing her head off. Charlie is there too."

"Marion Fields?" The first traces of belief were in Malcolm's voice.

"We still got a job here," said Roy.

"Not anymore," I answered. "Singh is dead. You're not working for him anymore. You're free, free to do what you want, not what Singh wants."

"Don' know," muttered Roy. "If you lie and we don' finish here, we in deep shit."

"Go check," I said. "Go."

Roy wavered. "I go look. Malcolm, you stay. Don' let he wife leave. If he try to take she out, kill she. I go see if he lie. I going to be quick."

"Not too quick," I told him. "You'll have to walk. There's no Fido or Birdbrain to give you a ride."

"Maybe I catch a taxi," he said, laughing softly. "Do some hum-bugging on the way."

"You'd better find some way to hurry," I said to Roy. "Jadine needs a doctor."

"If you lying, she need funeral home," Roy said. He left the house, heading for West Moorings.

"We ought to go ahead and finish job," said Malcolm.

"You don't seem to understand," I said to Malcolm. "This is my wife. Have your fun on your own from now on. Not because Singh orders it. Go after someone you really dislike, not a stranger you're ordered to dislike. Leave my wife and kids alone."

Malcolm looked startled, then thoughtful. "Maybe, if Mr. Singh really dead."

"He's dead," I said. "No doubt at all about that."

"Then, if he really dead, me and Roy have to do something about Mrs. Singh. You, too. Otherwise, she take over. Then we still caught. You say we free, but that true only if she dead, too. Anything less and we still trapped. So you help we get she, we let you wife go free. Deal?"

"Listen asshole, understand something," I growled. "You will let my wife and kids go free whether I help you or not. If you want me to help you on something, then ask, but don't threaten, don't bargain. Now, what is so damn important about Singh's wife that you want her dead? You are asking my help to kill her, right?"

"Truth! You in same boat like we. She find out she husband gone she grab we. You part of Mr. Singh's group, and he make sure she know all we. You already marked, man. More better you help we."

"Maybe," I answered, "but Jadine is hurt. You two hurt her, and she has to get to the hospital."

"Look man, Mrs. Singh she grab you and what you think going to happen to wife? I think you have to deal with we. No time to play game. Show we where she live. We do the heavy work, but we maybe need some help, too."

There appeared to be no room for argument. By the time Roy returned, time would be running out for all of us.

"I can show you where she lives," I said, "but I don't know her first name. Singh's name was Baal Ramish, so Ramish has to be her last name, too. I'll help, but first we have to get my wife some help."

"Talk 'bout you wife later. That last name not enough man. Need she real name. All of it."

"That I don't know," I said. "Maybe we can find something at her house. If not, maybe we can take her by surprise."

Malcolm looked doubtful. "Maybe. Okay, we wait for Roy to come back. If Mr. Singh dead, all we go hassle he wife and them. You, too. You don' have choice, just like we. And your wife go free. Deal?"

"No deal. My wife needs a doctor now."

He shrugged. "Just hope she got strength make phone call after Roy return. You lucky like hell. Couple minute more and all this talk no never mind. She lucky, man."

"We could set off the burglar alarm," I said. "I installed it before I died. That would bring help, and I could go with you."

"Maybe," he answered.

An hour passed, a second, and he was back.

"Yes, man, Mr. Singh he dead!" he announced. "We free! Clark tell the truth, man."

"Not free until Mrs. Singh dead," Malcolm told him. "Clark, he agree take us to she house."

"First my wife," I muttered. I was afraid Jadine would not have enough strength to use the phone. It had to be the burgler alarm. I went to it, glanced at Malcolm, who nodded. Quickly I activated it and listened in satisfaction to the strident wailing.

"All right, now let's go," I said. "With that racket, she's bound to get help."

"Wish you luck with she," said Malcolm, in what was probably the first compassionate response from him in several years.

"Thanks," I said. "Now let's take care of the rest of this affair."

Again I made the trip down the Diego Martin Main Road, still heavy with traffic at nine in the morning. This time, I was not alone.

We moved past Cocorite, through St. James, up Tragarete Road, and finally to the house I was in so short a while before. Singh's home.

By the time we arrived, I had determined that my decision to help them had been an absolute necessity. I was beginning to get the idea it might take more than just Malcolm and Roy to handle Singh's wife. If they were unsuccessful, she would be after me next. I had killed her husband, after all. She might feel a need for revenge, or might consider me a flawed tool to be discarded. Either way, I was involved, like it or not, and I had a stake in the outcome.

This woman must die, I realized, or everything has been in vain.

The house guard was still in place, but Malcolm did not seem upset in the least.

"Where the window Birdbrain fly you from?" he asked.

I pointed to it, and, sure enough, the break was still there. It could be seen. It was all that was needed.

We entered the house.

We found Mrs. Singh, or Mrs. Ramish, in her kitchen, preparing breakfast. She apparently did not know Singh was dead.

As we entered the kitchen, I heard a spitting sound, There, on a chair near the stove, was a pure black cat, its back arched, spitting in fury. It's eyes were locked on Malcolm and Roy, then it was off the chair and under the table.

Roy did not make the mistake I made with Singh. He entered the kitchen, located Mrs. Singh, picked up a knife, and stabbed her. At the last minute she moved, as if sensing something, and the knife went into her shoulder, not her heart.

She screamed, more in rage than from pain, and something grabbed Roy. It threw him down and ripped at him. Something unseen but no less real for that.

Then it was not unseen. It was the cat. At least it was black and feline in appearance, but much larger than the cat, and evil radiated from it. Singh had his Fido, and his wife had a cat beast of some kind, that was linked to her as Fido had been linked to Singh.

"A trick!" Malcolm howled. "She ready for we!"

He took a meat cleaver and went at her, swinging. He never reached her. She sensed him, this time I was sure she sensed him, and he joined Roy on the floor. The cat thing ate at them, noisily, actually consuming portions of their bodies as if they were real.

I stared, horrified. This woman was more dangerous than her husband. He talked. She acted.

I kept very quiet, hoping I would not be noticed. She laughed softly as she moved toward the telephone in the next room, blood dripping from her shoulder.

"Fools!" she snarled. "My husband is attacked in his own home, and you think I would be unprotected? You are fools."

She gazed at her pet as it fed, and if she didn't see Roy or Malcolm she sensed them so strongly that it didn't matter.

"Now, you pay," she said, "but, first, a doctor. If anything is left when I return, I'll chain it under the sea."

I followed her to the telephone. I heard something still ripping at Malcolm and Roy, and I heard their screams. I remained quiet, not willing to risk any attack in this house. I would just end up on the floor with Malcolm and Roy.

The phone table was near an old desk. I noticed a bunch of papers there. Curious, I looked through them. They were legal papers of various sorts, birth certificates and such. I looked again. Yes, they were getting passports. I found Singh's real name written out. Suddenly hopeful, I rummaged further.

There it was, among the rest of the papers, a birth certificate for Lalita Nanoo. So, after marriage, her real name was Lalita Ramish. I memorized it. Soon I would have a use for it.

Meanwhile, she had called her doctor. Then she called a taxi to meet her doctor. I joined her in the taxi.

Roy had been right in immediately stabbing her, but he had been careless. Now he was paying for that carelessness. I did not want to make that mistake when I made my move.

The taxi arrived at its destination quickly, such speed unusual in Trinidad, so I knew the Singhs had something going; perhaps as simple as the drivers wanting to be rid of frightening cargo as soon as possible.

The doctor was waiting, and the waiting room was empty. She was ushered into a small room for treatment.

Now! I thought, as the doctor left the room.

I moved toward her.

"I know you're here," she said, conversationally. "I still have protection with me, a nice little beastie. I'm afraid he has a vicious nature though."

I looked around wildly, saw nothing.

She laughed.

"You won't see my pet. He is similar to the one I left home with the other two fools. I have always been partial to cats, and my beasts know it. They use that guise to please me.

"Nice thing about cats, I can let them be visible to living people, and they think they're cute. Of course, I doubt if your friends appreciate that cuteness."

She looked straight at me, as if she saw me. "Now, you, you were smarter. You waited. You must be the American, the clever one. I told my husband not to keep you. Too intelligent."

She paused. "Enough," she said. "Once this fool doctor is done, I will take care of you. Unfinished business. My pet will hold you for me."

I leaped at her and caught her face in my hand. Something tore at my shoulder, pulling me back. In desperation, I lunged free, feeling part of my shoulder remaining behind. With the last of my strength I reached for her again.

She was laughing harder, her mouth open. In my brief moment of freedom, I took hold of her tongue. As I was pulled free, I attempted to tear her tongue from her mouth. I got part of it.

She screamed, blood flowing from her mouth. Her beast was still savaging me, trying to pull me away from her. I heard the sound of approaching footsteps. It had to be the doctor.

I got my good hand on a scalpel from the table and swiped at Mrs. Singh. Blood spurted from a new gash across her chest.

Not deep enough!

I groaned.

She was almost to the door and out of my reach when she was tripped. I heard a voice, "Now you die, like your husband."

In disbelief I saw Marion Fields had entered the room. The beast was still busy with me, so Marion had some freedom of action. She was trying to finish the job, choking, hitting, whatever. There had to be a spell of some kind, for it did not appear that Mrs. Singh was weakening at all.

In desperation, I ripped free of the cat thing, scuttled across the room and grabbed the scalpel once more. I moved closer to the struggling pair, avoiding the beast.

"Marion," I yelled. "Her name is Lalita Ramish."

Three times, I thought.

I looked at Mrs. Singh. "Lalita Ramish," I repeated. "You are Lalita Ramish." I tossed the scalpel to Marion. I then attacked the cat beast to give Marion time.

Marion jumped forward and put the scalpel in Mrs. Singh's eye and pushed. She was having no more problems. I could hear Mrs. Singh screaming as Marion finished with her. Once her immunity was gone, Mrs. Singh died quickly, and the cat thing was forced away, also.

I staggered to my feet and moved out the door, past the doctor who finally had entered and was staring in horror at his patient.

The death we had given Mrs. Singh was not a pretty death, and blood covered every wall in the room. Knowing what she was, I could imagine what the doctor was thinking, the fears that would now be forming in his head.

But he was safe. The monster was dead.

I left Marion there and returned home to find Jadine gone and a neighbor watching the children. Jadine was in the hospital. My fears returned. Was she found in time, or did she bleed to death? Would this terrible day never end?

Again, I raced down the streets to the Port of Spain hospital. It was not a long trip, but my imagination was furnishing me no end of vivid possibilities. The journey seemed endless. I had my freedom, but the price might have been too great.

Finally, I reached the hospital. I searched for almost an hour before I found her in an open ward, sleeping. Just sleeping. My relief was overwhelming.

The long, long day was nearly over.

I watched Jadine sleeping, and my heart yearned. At last, I entered her dream.

She was at our beach in Maracas, lying on a towel by the sea, crying and alone. I moved up slowly and made a small noise.

She looked up.

"Clark! The children?"

"Okay," I said. "They're okay. Jadine, I killed Singh, and Mrs. Singh is dead, too. The name was the weapon after all. It made the difference."

She started crying, and I took her in my arms and comforted her. "Is it really over?" she asked.

"Yes, it's over."

We held each other for a time, then she pulled clear and looked at me with fresh horror on her face.

"Clark, I try to stop they after I got here. I make they bring me phone and thing and I tried to stop they. I know maybe you won or I dead all now, so I tried to stop they."

I stopped the torrent of words by gently touching her lips with one finger.

"Stop who?" I asked.

"The Ministry of Health." she answered.

"So my body stays here?"

"No," she replied. "I too late. They exhume your body yesterday, early. Body on plane this morning, going to Barbados and then New

York. Elizabeth know and she going take it to Metuchin in New Jersey."

She was crying again. "Clark, it already gone, out of Trinidad."

I sat there, stunned. "Then I'll be forced to go," I said, "and now I don't want to."

"I call Elizabeth," decided Jadine.

"Forget it," I answered. "They would never allow it to be shipped back again. Neither government will allow that."

I knew I never wanted to leave Trinidad, but I would be given no choice. And, once gone, I could never return. She could follow me, of course, but that I could not bring myself to ask. Trinidad was her home, and I was dead. She would survive much easier here.

Then her medicine took her into a deeper sleep, and her dream ended. I was locked out.

She did not dream again that night.

By the next afternoon, I expected to be snapped away to the United States, and it would be over. I would be in New Jersey, where I did not want to be.

I wanted to stay home, and home was Trinidad. Home was Jadine.

I could not stay and watch her sleep, becoming more and more depressed. I decided to check Singh one last time, before I had to leave, a reassurance thing; a desire to know Jadine would be safe once I was no longer here. The long walk to West Moorings might help me get my thinking back in gear. The long walk did not help.

I moved along the shore at West Moorings and reached the place where so much had happened.

Charlie was gone, Singh's heart was gone, and, suddenly, I knew he had come back for his heart. I shuddered, sat and worried. There was no one to care.

I did not get to talk to Jadine again. I was forced away, back to the States.

CHAPTER TWENTY THREE

It was a gray, overcast February day in 1983 before I had enough strength to leave the cemetery in Metuchin. Snow flew, and there was slush on the streets. Still despondent, I moved out onto the street by the cemetery. The day fit my mood, the same mood that had adhered to me since my return to the States.

My thoughts dwelt on Jadine constantly as I wandered aimlessly through Metuchin, going nowhere, just wandering, a lost soul. I was constantly tormented by my memories of those last moments with her, wishing I had asked her to come with me, knowing I did not have the right to ask. I had little hope she might come, but a great many regrets. It had already been months since our parting.

By May my strength was fully returned, and I convinced myself it was time to stop wandering and time to see what I could see in my new home.

I determined to visit my daughters and my grandson. A tiny ray of hope remained that, maybe, they could send for Jadine. It was only a tiny hope, because Elizabeth had never liked her and still resented the fact that I left Jadine the bulk of my money. Nonetheless, that tiny hope was all I had left.

I went into Elizabeth's home, stayed a week, and watched her with Carrie and little Daniel.

It was not the same. I wanted to be home with Jadine and my children. New Jersey was not my home, not now, not for a long while.

I stayed longer, unable to bring myself to leave. In the fifth week, a letter came from Jadine, and I managed to read it over Elizabeth's shoulder. She said she was moving to the States, permanently. She asked Elizabeth to find her a house in the Metuchin area, so she could be close to the cemetery and me. The move was planned for August, before school started.

I sighed, gratefully. It was over.

With Jadine here, I could be satisfied, even happy for what time remained to me in this world. When Jadine got here, I would be home at last.